MW01437847

Colors of Time

Laurie Jones

Hard Shell Word Factory

To Mom and Dad, the solid foundation in my life.
Love, always,

And eternal gratitude to my friend and inspirational writing mentor,
Judy Griffith Gill.

Copyright 1999 Laurie Jones
ISBN: 1-58200-503-6
Published December 1999

Trade paperback
ISBN-10: 0-7599-0276-3
ISBN-13: 978-0-7599-0276-3
Published December 2007

Hard Shell Word Factory
PO Box 161
Amherst Jct. WI 54407
books@hardshell.com
www.hardshell.com
All rights reserved.

All characters in this book have no existence outside the imagination of the author, and have no relation whatever to anyone bearing the same name or names. These characters are not even distantly inspired by any individual known or unknown to the author, and all incidents are pure invention.

Prologue

JONATHAN WILKS fanned the cards slowly, keeping his hand close to his chest. No man could be trusted to be above cheating when the stakes were so high. In only ten short months he had become a player to reckon with at the twice-weekly round of poker in the smoky back room of the Deighton Hotel.

A plume of pungent cigar smoke floated past Jonathan's face as he rearranged his hand, then eyed the last of his six opponents, 'Gassy Jack' Deighton.

Tension ran high as the pile of money grew in front of Jonathan. There was at least two thousand dollars, maybe more. Whatever, he knew it would be enough to get started with his new life, and his new bride. By this time tomorrow, Margaret Marie Hollister would be his, and his alone.

Despite what her family thought of him, Margaret had pledged her love to him a fortnight ago. Nothing would keep them apart now. He had sealed his promise to her by offering one half of a gold shilling, cut with a zigzag design into two pieces. Scottie, the local goldsmith, had done a fine job indeed. Each half had been bored with a small hole, and Margaret's put on a delicate gold chain, while Jonathan's hung by a serviceable thong of the finest leather.

Margaret had shed tears of joy when he'd presented the gift of engagement to her. They'd met secretly on the shores of the inlet. The moon had shone on the cobalt blue waters as if it lighting the path to their future. A thousand stars had twinkled above. She'd made him the happiest man on earth that night, and tomorrow they were to elope.

Jonathan and Margaret Wilks. Even their names fit together like....

"Mr. Wilks!"

Jonathan was jolted away from his thoughts abruptly as Robert Bold, the dealer in tonight's game asked, apparently for a second time, "How many cards, or are ya just gonna sit there with that stupid grin on yer face?"

Gassy Jack stared from across the table, his face unflinching.

"Grinnin' like Crazy Louis, he is. Ain't never gonna be a good poker player like that," said a slightly drunken man from somewhere behind Jonathan. William Smith, Jonathan thought, preparing to discard. Worst poker player in town, and he had the audacity to make a comment like that. *Well, William, you old fool, your money is part of this lovely pile as well,* Jonathan thought smugly.

He tossed two cards, face down, towards the dealer. "Two, my good man," Jonathan said, laying on his thickest British accent. The smile never left his face. Let them think what they will. He may be just a remittance man, shipped unceremoniously to this God forsaken collection of wood planks called Gastown, but his blood ran deep through generations of pure English nobility. One day he would give Margaret the castle and all the riches she deserved. He loved her with all of his heart and soul.

Jonathan placed the two cards he had been dealt back into his hand, and while he tried to put on a 'poker face', he beamed inwardly. A royal flush—a most fitting hand, he thought.

"Right, then. I'll open with one dollar," he said, tossing a coin into the centre of the green, felt-covered table.

Jack Deighton eyed Jonathan briefly, then with the briefest of movement, tossed a coin to the table centre. "I'll see your dollar and raise you five," he replied, adding a five dollar note.

Jonathan was filled with the courage of love. Tonight was his night to triumph—over this game and over the threats of Margaret's wealthy father, James Hollister.

"I'll see your five and raise you twenty more!"

Jack twisted his moustache thoughtfully. "I'll see your twenty and raise you one hundred dollars." Again, with only the slightest of movement, he reached for his diminishing pile of money, and tossed several notes to the centre of the table.

A murmur of anticipation rumbled about the small, smoke-filled room. Jonathan held Jack Deighton's gaze as someone snickered, followed by an immediate shushing from another. A thick hush enveloped the players and observers.

Jonathan stared across the table at his opponent, oblivious to the new round of murmuring slowly rising from the onlookers. The room crackled with anticipation. Somewhere, a clock ticked off the seconds as Jonathan closed his fan of cards, leaned forward and retrieved one hundred dollars from his stash.

Nonchalantly, he tossed it over the growing pile. "I'll see your hundred and raise you..." Jonathan looked at his rather large pot of winnings, then with Margaret's smile filling his mind, he counted out several bills. "I will raise you five hundred more, Mr. Deighton. Now, will it be your round of whiskey, or mine?"

"Only a drunkard or a fool would place a wager like that, Mr. Wilks. But since I'm in a mood of good humour tonight, I'll pay for the next round out of all that cash you're willing to throw away." He reached for his stack of bills, peeled off several and tossed them onto the table. "Call. Let's see what you're made of son."

The crowd looked at Jonathan with anticipation. He smiled as he laid his hand down. "Royal flush, I do believe," he said quietly.

"Damn," was all Jack Deighton said as he threw his cards on the table.

The crowd erupted with a chorus of hoots and whistles. Jonathan reached triumphantly for his winnings as well-wishers slapped him on the back.

Deighton rose slowly from his chair. Uttering a quiet note of congratulations, he walked to the front of the saloon.

Jonathan accepted the salutation with a smile. "Better luck next time, old boy!" he said as he stuffed the money into his stained, leather satchel bag. To nobody in particular, he said, "I'd have to sell a lot of my paintings to equal this!"

"Nobody wants your ugly paintings, Wilks! Why don't you just write home to your rich mommy and daddy if you need money so bad," Stanley Miller said sarcastically.

"Very funny, Stanley. When my paintings are hanging in the finest galleries, you'll surely be singing another tune." The crowd of onlookers had almost cleared as Jonathan stood from the table and retrieved his overcoat from the curved peg on the wall. He bowed theatrically to those who remained. "Gentlemen, it's been a pleasure," he said as he slung his bag over his shoulder and walked out the back door with a bounce in his step. He stopped for a moment, looked up to the stars and smiled.

Jonathan whistled a tune as he walked along the back lane, the Hollister Rooming House only a short block away. He heartily enjoyed the fact that, although Margaret's father disapproved of him, James Hollister was also greedy and did not want to lose a wealthy, or at least the son of a wealthy family, as a long-term guest.

As Jonathan reached for the back door to the rooming house, he heard someone run up from behind. He turned to see who was there, and felt a sudden, sharp pain in the back of his head. He felt himself crumple against the door, and his world went black.

Chapter 1

KATE CARSTON was exhausted, mind numb from yet another sleepless night. She sat in her favourite over-stuffed wingback chair and stared at the half restored painting sitting on the antique easel. It broke her heart to part with it. There were only four left after this one. A part of her history would belong to the highest bidder.

She took a long sip on her coffee, and looked towards the beams of early morning sunlight filtering through the stained-glass window over the front door of her gallery. She smiled sadly. The delicate pieces of colored glass had seen many beautiful sunrises for over one hundred and twenty-five years. Grandmother Margaret would surely turn in her grave if she knew what was happening to her home.

Kate shrugged off the gloomy thoughts, placed her coffee mug on a nearby table and stood. She stretched lazily, willing her tired mind to continue the painstaking task of restoring the Jonathan Wilks painting.

A sudden thud at the back door startled her. She looked at the grandfather clock at the bottom of the staircase nearby. Seven-thirty. Too early for Jenny, her assistant. Too late, much too late for the last wave of drunks leaving O'Malley's Pub down the block.

Kate walked to the door, ensuring it was still locked securely, and listened for a sign of anyone outside. She heard a groan, and the old knob rattled. Someone was trying to get in!

"Who's there?" Kate shouted through the solid oak door.

"Margaret? Is that you, my love? Why is the door locked?" came a strange man's voice, thick with an English accent.

"We're closed until nine o'clock," Kate shouted again.

"Margaret, darling, please. I'm in need of medical attention," he replied.

Margaret? Who was he talking to? Maybe he was hurt though. Kate cautiously opened the door slightly, keeping the heavy security chain in place. She drew in her breath sharply. The man was bleeding—some sort of gash on the top of his head. The blood had run down over one side of his face, and he was writhing in pain, his eyes shut tightly as he leaned against the brick wall of the gallery.

Still keeping the chain affixed, she asked, "What happened?"

Not opening his eyes, he reached toward her voice. "Someone...I didn't see them...oh no! My bag!" He dropped to his hands and knees and began frantically searching the ground around him, his eyes still half closed by the blood. "Margaret! Someone has stolen my bag!"

Margaret who? Kate wondered. She closed the door to undo the chain. By the time she opened the door again, the stranger had succumbed to the blow on his head. He was out cold, lying three-quarters prone in the doorway.

"Great. Just great," Kate muttered aloud. She quickly ran to the office and grabbed her cordless phone, punching in 9-1-1 as she hurried back to the door.

"Yes, uh, I'd like to report a man who is bleeding, and, I hope, just passed out at the back door of my gallery...yes...uh, yes, he's breathing. I think he was mugged. He was ranting on about some bag being gone...yes...the back door in the Alley...Blood Alley in Gastown...#87...yes, that's right...Carston Gallery. Okay...thank you."

Kate tried to recall her limited First Aid knowledge. Let's see...breathing? Yes. Coherent? Definitely not. Restrictive clothing? No, but dressed oddly.

She noted his long, dark brown suede coat, very well tailored. An expensive white linen shirt and gray wool pants indicated he had good taste. A different style than she had noticed lately, though. His blood-caked, jet-black hair was shoulder length, and covered his face as he lay there. He almost looked as if he has just come from the set of the old west film that was being shot in the Valley.

Kate heard the wail of an ambulance approaching. She shook his arm lightly. "Hey, wake up! Are you okay?" Her efforts were rewarded with another moan, and a slight stirring from the once lifeless figure.

As the ambulance drove slowly into the alley, Kate stepped over the stranger and waved down the paramedics.

One of the attendants rushed to Kate's doorway as his partner retrieved the medical kit.

"So, what do we have here?" he asked, bending down to the victim. Kate noted his nametag—Belton.

"I heard a thud at the door and this is what I found," Kate said, watching as Belton rolled the stranger carefully on to his back and began to examine the cut on his head.

"Do you know him?" he asked.

"No," Kate replied, but as the paramedics worked on him, she took a good look at the man's face. A memory stirred inside her. He was very handsome. Something *was* familiar about him. Where had she seen him before?

The man reached consciousness with a start as Belton's partner, Krower, held smelling salts under his nose.

"Hey, hey, take it easy there buddy. We're trying to help you. What's your name?" Krower asked.

The man leaned against the wall, his eyes closed tightly against the pain in his head. "My name is Jonathan Wilks, of course! Everyone in Gastown knows who I..." He stopped abruptly as he opened his eyes and looked first at the two paramedics, then at the ambulance, then at Kate.

He quickly put his hands up in defense. "Who are you...? What are you? Where am I?" He looked up at Kate. "Margaret...you're not Margaret! Who are you?"

His eyes were riveting. Blue as a Rocky Mountain lake, and at the moment, just as cold. Kate felt her stomach clench as he stared at her.

This was some kind of joke. It had to be. Kate stood frozen in the doorway, her hand over her mouth in stunned silence. Jonathan Wilks? Obviously it wasn't *the* Jonathan Wilks. He died in 1868. But the clothes...the English accent...and he had been calling for Margaret. No. This wasn't, couldn't be happening. There had to be an explanation.

"Hey, buddy, it's okay. You got a nasty bump on the head. Where do you live?" Belton asked, trying to calm him.

"I...I...I live here," he said weakly, looking at the doorway where Kate stood, still silent. "I live at the Hollister Rooming House, but...I...I'm not feeling well..." he murmured as he passed out again.

"No, it can't be," Kate said quietly. The Hollister Rooming House. Margaret Hollister. The maiden name of her great, great, great grandmother. Who was this man?

As Krower reached for the smelling salts again, Belton looked up at Kate. "Hey, are you okay? You look white as a ghost." He noticed she was staring at the unconscious patient. "Are you sure you don't know this guy?"

"I don't think so, but, uh, there's something familiar." she stammered, unable to collect her thoughts.

Krower had loosened the top buttons on the man's shirt. "Well, it looks like you two have one thing in common."

Kate tried not to notice the mat of dark, curly hair framed by the opening of his white shirt.

"What?" she asked, her mind still racing. What if he was...*him.*

"Seems like you both shop at the same jewelry store," he said, lifting the jagged gold piece on the leather thong around the man's neck.

Kate gasped as her hand flew to the open neckline of her blouse. His pendant was identical to the piece that hung from a delicate gold chain around her neck. But hers was one of a kind, or so she thought. A treasured family heirloom that had been passed down through the female descendants from Grandmother Margaret. *Margaret.* He had been calling for Margaret.

The story of the pendants' origin had been one of purest romance. Although no one knew the complete extent of the courtship, there was a family story of a great love between Grandmother Margaret and Jonathan Wilks. It was a secret that Margaret almost took to her grave. No one knew, or hadn't dared breathe a word, until her granddaughter, Lucy Monroe, Kate's great, great grandmother, had inherited the gold piece that Kate now wore. In her will, Grandmother Margaret led the family to a false bottom in a desk drawer, where she had hidden the necklace for over sixty years.

Along with it had been a letter. Part of it read, 'Jonathan Wilks, rest his soul, was my first and only true love. A collection of his paintings is in the locked strongbox in the darkest corner of the attic. I am entrusting you, Lucy, to keep this gold piece, and the collection of paintings in the family, and may you, and all of the women who follow in our family, find your true love—a love that is as deep as my love was for Jonathan'.

Kate shook herself back to reality. Belton was talking to her, but she hadn't heard a thing he'd said.

"...and if he doesn't want to go..."

"Uh, sorry, what did you say?" Kate asked, still not quite sure if she was in some kind of a waking dream.

"I said the bump on his head looks worse than it is. I don't think he'll even need stitches, but we should take him into Emerg in case he has a concussion. If he doesn't want to go, though, he'll have to sign a release form."

"Come on John, buddy, wake up!" Krower said loudly. "Yeah, that's it. You'll be okay. Do you want to go to the hospital?"

Jonathan groaned, holding on to his head. "All I want is for you people to tell me where the devil I am, and what is going on here. And quit shouting! I'm not bloody deaf!"

Kate had to think fast. The possibility of him being *the* Jonathan Wilks was absolutely ludicrous, but how else would all of the other pieces fit? The English accent, saying he lived at the Hollister Rooming House, a name for which her gallery had not been known for over seventy years, and asking for Margaret. Unless he was some sort of dedicated historian, or a psychic, that information was just not common knowledge. And the pendant. How could he possibly have the matching piece?

"Where did you say you were from, sir?" Kate asked 'Jonathan', stalling for time.

"Well, I'm from England, of course, but..."

"Oh, my goodness, you must be my *cousin* Jonathan. *Aunt Margaret* wrote me about the possibility of you looking me up," she improvised quickly. If by some stroke of cruel fate, he was who he said he was, it was very bad timing. She was up to her eyeballs with the mortgage problem right now. Falling into a real life episode of *Unsolved Mysteries* was just not something she needed.

"Look guys," Kate said to the paramedics, "if you think that all he has is a slight concussion, then he really doesn't need to go to the hospital, does he?" She hoped they would just do their job and leave.

"Not really, but are you sure this is the guy you think it is? This isn't exactly the sanest part of town, if you know what I mean," Belton replied with concern.

"Bloody hell!" Jonathan shouted, still sitting on the ground as Krower cleaned his wound and applied a large bandage.

"Well, he did say someone had stolen his bag, and since I think the only way he could have the matching necklace would be if it was passed on in the family, then yes, I would tend to think that this is the guy. I'm sure it'll be okay. Besides, my assistant will be here in fifteen minutes or so. I'll be fine. Maybe you can just help get him to the sofa in the back office of my gallery."

The paramedics lifted Jonathan to his feet, but his legs gave way almost immediately. After a second try, he stood for a moment, getting his balance and leaned heavily on the men who half carried him inside. Kate noticed that Jonathan was tall, over six feet. His calf length suede coat opened to reveal a very lean, obviously fit man. Even in his present state, he exuded an air of refinement.

They carefully set Jonathan on the sofa in Kate's office, and took one more look at the bandaged bump on his head.

"He should be okay. Maybe you can make sure he doesn't go to sleep for a while, just in case," said Krower, closing his medical kit.

"No problem," Kate replied, sitting at the other end of the sofa. "Thanks for your help."

Belton turned to Jonathan, who was looking around the office, a deep frown etching his features.

"Just sign on the dotted line here, John, and we'll be on our way. You're sure you don't want to go to the hospital?"

Jonathan looked up at him, seemingly dazed. "No. No, I don't want to go anywhere. I just want to get back to the Hollister Rooming House," he said quietly. He took the ballpoint pen offered, and turned it over several times, staring at its strange configuration. He looked at the page, where the paramedic was pointing to the signature line, then started looking around the area.

"What's wrong, John? Just sign here, buddy," Belton said, with practiced patience.

Jonathan looked around again. "If you would kindly pass me the ink, I shall be happy to sign."

The paramedics looked questioningly at Kate. "I think we have a slight problem here, ma'am. It may not be such a good idea to leave him here alone with you," Krower said.

Kate hesitated, wondering what she should do. She had to find out who this guy was, not that she believed in any of that metaphysical junk. She'd never even given in to having her tealeaves read by Clarice, the psychic at the coffee shop across the street. But something was drawing her toward this man. Something very familiar, almost comforting.

She burst into laughter, false even to her own ears. "Oh, that's funny! Aunt Margaret said that you were the comedian of the family. Look, uh, *Jonathan*, just press hard with that pen. You'll do fine," she continued her fake laugh.

All three of the men in her office looked at her as if she'd lost her mind, too, but Jonathan slowly took her advice, pressing hard as the letter "J" rolled on to the paper. He stopped, looked at the end of the pen, then back at the paper, and smiled.

"My goodness, this is extraordinary!" He finished signing his name, although his hand shook visibly, and sat back to admire his handiwork. "What an exceptional instrument! I must have one!"

The paramedics looked at each other and shook their heads. "Keep it," Belton said, chuckling. "Welcome to Canada."

"I would pay you, but I'm afraid someone has..."

"Stolen your bag. Yeah, we know," Belton finished. "Ma'am, are you sure you don't want us to take him with us?"

Kate smiled. "No, uh, Aunt Margaret said he was a bit eccentric, but harmless. Don't worry. I'll figure this out. He's obviously not in any shape to do a lot of damage. I'll be fine. Thanks again for your help."

"No problem," they replied in unison.

"Call us if he changes his mind, or has any further problems," Belton said as they went out the back door.

"Thanks. Bye." Kate waved and closed the door, leaning against it. What on earth was going on here? Kate considered herself an open-minded woman, and Lord knows there were a lot of unexplained phenomenon in the world, but this...

She pushed away from the door and walked into her office. Maybe this was just a practical joke. Or a dream. No. There he was. Big as life. And just as handsome as she could have ever imagined in all the years that he had been her imaginary prince. He was leaning forward, his elbows resting on his knees as he held his bandaged head in his hands. Another groan escaped.

"Madam, if you don't mind, would you please explain to me where I am? I'm afraid I'm just a little confused."

Kate sat down on the sofa again, and sighed, her hands clasping and unclasping in her lap. She looked at him for a long moment, trying to gather her thoughts.

"Okay," she began. "Let's get one or two things straight. First, what is your real name?"

Jonathan slowly looked up at her, really looked at her. She was dressed as a man, quite unbecoming in dungarees, but quite beautiful at the same time. Her hair fell about her shoulders, long and golden, not unlike Margaret's. He longed to feel the silky strands fall through his fingers.

But something was wrong. Terribly wrong. His last recollection was of walking back from the poker game, his fortune securely held in his shoulder bag, and then...then...He looked at the woman sitting on the sofa. His name. She had asked him his name.

"My name is Jonathan Wilks. And who, may I ask, Madam, are you?" A thought suddenly occurred to him. "Have I been kidnapped?"

"Kidnapped?" Kate laughed. "No, you have not been kidnapped. And you obviously aren't *the* Jonathan Wilks. Are you one of his descendants from England?"

"I assure you, Madam, I am, as you say, *the* Jonathan Wilks, and as far as I can recollect, I have no relatives of the same name, though my uncle went by the name James." He sighed deeply, and continued. "As I'm sure you are aware, my family is of considerable wealth, not to mention nobility, however, since they unceremoniously shipped me off to this uncivilized part of the world, I hardly think they should be interested in paying a handsome reward for my safe return."

There was definitely something not right here. Maybe she shouldn't have suggested he be left here with her, alone. "You have not been kidnapped, at least not by me. Now, let's try this one more time, before I do call the police. Who are you?"

"Police? But it is I who was robbed! My bag had over two thousand dollars in it! Now Margaret and I..." He stopped abruptly. "Margaret. She'll be frantic that I haven't come to fetch her. We were to..." Again he stopped, realizing that he almost gave away the secret of their elopement.

"Well, forgive me, but due to the fact that Jonathan Wilks died over one hundred years ago, I'm sure there's some other explanation."

Died? Jonathan felt a sickening knot develop in his stomach. This must be a place in the afterworld. That would explain his strange surroundings—the odd way this woman was dressed, the pen that needed no ink, the carriage belonging to the men who had aided him. It was said that we see the ones we loved once we pass on. That must also explain how this woman resembled his beloved Margaret. He was in heaven. And this beautiful creature before him, tempting his desires, was an angel. He looked around the room again. It was familiar, almost like the rooming house, yet different. Yes, he must be in heaven.

But if he had died, why was he in so much pain? He gingerly touched the bandage on his head. No, he was sure he was not dead, however, he did not feel well. Not well at all.

"I assure you. I am Jonathan Wilks, and I may have gone over a gentleman's limit in whiskey at the Deighton Hotel last night, but..."

"The Deighton Hotel?" Kate almost whispered.

Grandmother Margaret's secret letter had said that the night before she and Jonathan Wilks were to elope, he had won a lot of money playing poker at the Deighton Hotel, according to other men in town. Not that *they* had lost any money to him, for they had given sincere promises to their wives that they would stay away from "Gassy Jack" Deighton's gaming table.

Something had happened to Jonathan after that game, her letter had read, because he never came back to the Hollister Rooming House. Nobody ever saw him again. Grandmother Margaret had been distraught for weeks. She took all of the items that belonged to Jonathan, his clothes, his paintings, a photo of the two of them at the spring carnival, and locked them away. The photo!

"Stay here...don't move," Kate said as she jumped to her feet, and started towards the doorway of her office. "I'll be back in one minute."

Jonathan looked up at her, bewildered. Every move sent daggers of pain through his head. Of course he wasn't going anywhere. Although he was beginning to wonder if this woman was completely mad! She was very much mistaken if she and her accomplices had any notion of grand financial gains at his expense.

A moment later, the she burst into the room again, holding in her hand an oval framed photograph. Jonathan watched as she looked from the photo to him, then back to the photo, then back to him. This procedure went on several more times, the look on her face changing from questioning to an expression of awe.

"Madam, what in heaven's name are you on about?" Jonathan asked exasperatedly.

Kate felt the blood drain from her face. She answered slowly, almost reverently. "You even have the same shoes on," she said. "You're Jonathan Wilks."

Jonathan raised one hand and looked upward, the motion once more sending spears of pain through his head.

"Thank goodness. I don't know what is in your hand that has opened your mind to the truth, but..."

Kate handed him the oval frame, and stood back to gauge his reaction. She saw his expression drop as he looked at the photograph of himself, standing stoically beside Grandmother Margaret.

"Madam, this photograph belongs to my Margaret. How did you come upon it?"

"Margaret is my great, great, great grandmother."

Chapter 2

JONATHAN STARED at the photograph as if in a trance. He gently ran one finger over Margaret's face below the glass.

"Margaret," he whispered. His eyes rose to meet Kate's. She sat on the couch and slowly began clasping and unclasping her hands again. Jonathan felt numb. This couldn't be happening. This just wasn't possible. People just didn't jump from one time to another. He needed answers, but could not find his voice. His mouth opened, then closed again in silence.

"Well, don't just sit there," Kate urged. "Say something!"

Jonathan looked at the photo again, then leaned back into the sofa. "And what would you have me say, madam? What a frightfully grand adventure! My beloved Margaret is dead, and I'm sitting on the sofa with one of her descendants! What fun! By the by, you seem to be avoiding the subject of your name."

"Kate," she said, crossing her arms and looking at him intently. "Kate Carston. And, not that I'm sure I believe this is all happening, but what I'd like to know is how you ended up at the back door of my gallery?"

"Madam...Miss Carston, I can assure you that I am at a complete loss as to how I came to be at your back door. As I have explained several times already, the last thing I remember is walking home to the Hollister Rooming House from an evening, a very profitable evening I might add, of gaming at the Deighton Hotel, when I was struck from behind." He gingerly, touched his bandaged head. "I reached for the door and..." his voice faltered, trying to come up with the next piece of the story.

Kate decided to play along. He seemed harmless enough so far. How she was going to explain this man to Jenny when she arrived was another problem, but she decided to take one step at a time. As bizarre as the situation was, if it was really happening, it certainly would be an interesting diversion from the anxiety of her financial problems.

"Okay," Kate began. "What year is it?"

"Well, if I was to answer truthfully, I would have to say it is 1868, but obviously it is not. The strange carriage that the medical men came in, the pen that does not require an ink pot," he rambled, pausing to take a long look at Kate from head to toe. "And most noticeably, our fine women of 1868 do not dress like...like...that!" he said, waving his hand up and down, focusing on her slim, denim-clad legs. "A lady does not wear dungarees!"

Kate looked down at her outfit. Dungarees? "Well, you're right. This is not 1868, it is 2007, and ladies can wear whatever..."

"What did you say?" Jonathan exclaimed in astonishment.

"I said, women of today can wear whatever they please and..."

"No, no, no! What year did you say it was?" Jonathan asked impatiently.

Kate stopped abruptly and looked over at him for a long moment. "The year is 2007. Are you sure you're not some Candid Camera stunt man or something?"

"I cannot answer that as I have not the faintest idea to what you might be referring." He looked around the room again. "Am I, or am I not at the Hollister Rooming House?" he demanded.

Kate paused. "This building *used* to be the Hollister Rooming House. It has been in my family for four generations. I'm the last in line. It was turned into a store by my great grandfather in the 1950's, and I inherited it five years ago when my mother died. Now it's known as Carston Gallery."

Jonathan looked around again. "But what of my Margaret? Obviously if you are her descendent, she must have wed and had children of her own. But if I am here, and I do not recall going through with our plans to wed, who won her heart?"

"According to the letters she wrote with her will, Jonathan Wilks was her one and only true love. She kept the necklace hidden from her family."

For the first time, Jonathan noticed the delicate gold chain around Kate's slender neck, which held his engagement present to Margaret. He just stared, his hand involuntarily reaching to his own pendant.

Kate reached behind her neck, lifting her hair to unclasp the precious heirloom, and handed it to Jonathan. He silently took it, then carefully slid the leather thong over his head, and brought the two pieces of gold together. They fit as snugly as if they had just been cut yesterday. He stared at the coin with a look that melted any doubt in Kate's mind that he was not who he said he was. His expression was a mixture of love, sadness and reverence.

Not speaking directly to her, Jonathan said, "Why? Why did this have to happen?" He looked up at Kate, his expression turning to confusion. "Why am I here, in this time? How did I get here?"

Kate shrugged. "Like I said, you tell me. I don't believe in all of this psychic hocus pocus." She heard a rumbling sound. "Sounds like one of us is hungry. I assume since you're British you'd like a cup of tea?"

"Yes, that would be most appreciated. Is there someone to whom I might speak who could shed some light on the mystery of my being here?" Jonathan asked, once again staring at the two gold pieces in his hands.

"Sure. I'll just call up the Psychic Friends Network, and waste $3.99 a minute trying to explain to them that someone dropped in at my back door from one hundred and forty odd years ago. Maybe they'll know!" Kate replied sarcastically.

"Thank you, I'd appreciate that. Then we might..."

"I was only kidding! If I did that they would lock me up, then I'd lose the gallery for sure."

"What do you mean, lose the gallery?" Jonathan asked.

"Never mind. That's my problem. Are you well enough to walk? You may be more comfortable in the gallery lounge. That's where my tea supplies are."

"I believe I'm fine," Jonathan replied, carefully standing up. He stood fully upright and wavered slightly. Kate quickly went to his side and took his arm. He was an extraordinarily handsome man. He smelled of cigar smoke and spicy cologne, and a faint odor of bourbon. He had what Kate envisioned as a typical English nobleman's build, tall and lean. She could feel the long length of muscle in his forearm tense as she helped him walk. His nearness was quite unnerving, and Kate felt a strange longing to be held by this man.

They walked together slowly out of Kate's back office and into the main gallery room. Jonathan stopped abruptly and stared toward the picture window at the front of the gallery. Cars and people whizzed past in the busy rush hour.

Kate noticed the puzzled, and somewhat frightened look on his face. As if reading his thoughts, she said, "You're right. Things are different now."

"Yes, quite," he replied quietly. Jonathan's gaze roamed the interior of the gallery. "My Lord! The ceiling is missing?" he cried out, once again leaning on Kate for support.

Kate's hand instinctively went to the broad expanse of his chest as he fought to maintain his balance. "It's not missing," she replied, laughing. "I had the room renovated for a loft effect. It gives me more space to show off my clients' works. It cost me a fortune to do it though, and now..."

"What do you mean your clients' works?"

"Artists. My customers. This is an art gallery. I show and sell works from artists from all over British Columbia," Kate said proudly. Reluctantly, she moved away from the warmth of his arm, once she assured herself he was steady enough to stand on his own.

Jonathan spotted the grandfather clock at the foot of the stairway next. "That clock! Margaret's father bought that clock for the family just after I arrived in Gastown!"

"If you look around enough, I'm sure you'll find lots of things like that. Grandfather Trueman was somewhat of a pack rat," Kate said as she plugged in the kettle and plopped two tea bags into a beautiful hand-painted antique china teapot.

Jonathan whirled to face her, a movement that almost sent him to his knees. He held his throbbing head as he walked toward Kate. "Trueman? Did you say Trueman? What has that name got to do with your family?" he asked.

Kate popped a crumpet in the toaster, something she usually saved for afternoon tea for one exclusive customer that visited weekly. It was the only thing on hand she had to feed her unexpected guest.

"Trueman was Grandmother Margaret's married name. She married a man by the name of Donovan Trueman. He was quite..."

"He is an arrogant, cheating bastard was what he is...was!" Jonathan almost spat out the words. "Are you trying to tell me that my precious, innocent Margaret married that cad?"

Kate crossed her arms in a defiant stance, taken aback by his outburst. "I'll thank you not to insult my family. Donovan Trueman was a very wealthy and respected businessman in old Gastown. You can look him up in any local history book in the library if you want."

Jonathan snorted. "Wealthy? The man doesn't have two shillings to rub together. Anything he had he always lost at Mr. Deighton's tables. He has nothing!"

Kate shrugged, turning her attention to selecting a jam to serve with the crumpet. "Well, according to history, and a few family stories, he came into a large inheritance, and started his own business importing fine china from England," she said, pointing to the antique teapot on the counter. "A few months after he received the inheritance, he and Margaret were married. I'm not sure whether Margaret ever really loved him, but her father approved immensely and, so the story goes, Margaret really had no choice in the matter. Obviously you weren't friends with the man."

"Friends? I despise him! I knew that he had an eye for Margaret, but he also had an eye for many of the young ladies in Gastown. Cad! That's all I can say about him. A cad! As far as I know, he did not have any relatives in Gastown. Where did the inheritance come from?"

"I don't know. But it was enough to impress James Hollister into giving his daughter's hand away in marriage."

"It was him," Jonathan said quietly, coming to the realization that Donovan Trueman had been the cause of the surreal situation he now faced. "He stole my money, and he stole my life."

"You don't know that, although..." Kate looked away, knowing that in all probability Jonathan was right.

Jonathan then noticed Kate's little galley kitchen. She was rinsing the knife she had just used to butter his crumpet. "Amazing! What a splendid collections of utensils. I dare say the women I know, that is of my... time," he struggled with the word, "would trade anything for an item such as this," he said as he lifted the whistling electric kettle.

Kate unplugged the kettle and gently extracted it from his hands. "You haven't seen anything yet, Mr. Wilks." She poured hot water into the china teapot, then handed him a plate with the strawberry jam laden crumpet. "Come on, let's get you off your feet again. You don't look well."

She motioned Jonathan toward the sofa next to her working area at the side of the gallery. As he walked toward it, he stopped abruptly in front of the easel that held his painting that Kate was restoring.

"Uh-oh," Kate whispered, reaching to take the antique plate from his hands before it went crashing to the hardwood floor.

Jonathan walked slowly towards the easel, staring at his own work, his arms limp by his side. He turned to Kate. She was beginning to feel very sorry for him. This was indeed, for whatever reason, a man out of his time. She wondered how she would handle the situation if she was in his place.

He slowly pointed at the easel. "This is my painting. Nobody wanted my paintings, well, except for my Margaret. How on earth..."

Kate took Jonathan by the arm and guided him to the sofa. She was once again vividly aware of a sense of familiarity, as if she had known him very well. As if she had once been very close to him. She tried to shake off the feeling.

"Sit. Eat. I'll try to explain what I can." She poured two cups of tea. "Sugar and milk?" she asked.

Jonathan stared at the painting. "No, clear is fine, thank you. I am thoroughly confused now, Miss Carston. I painted that piece just two weeks ago. It was barely dry."

"You can call me Kate. And I have a surprise for you, Mr. Wilks, that painting is over one hundred and thirty years old. We didn't have an exact date for it, but I guess now I do. I was just in the middle of touching it up."

"What do you mean touching it up? It was a finished piece," he said indignantly.

"I know, but it was quite faded, and it needed some work to bring it back. I am an art restoration expert by trade. It's a service I provide through my gallery. Obviously you are not aware of it, Mr. Wilks, but..."

"Jonathan. Please call me Jonathan," he asked, taking a long sip of tea.

"Very well, Jonathan," Kate continued. "Your works are worth a lot of money. Although they were passed down through the family after Margaret died, I've regretfully had to sell a couple of pieces in the last two months to take care of the mortgage. When you disappeared, someone decided that you had talent after all. Although Margaret gathered as many of your paintings as she could and hid them away, a few were found and, like all great, but dead, artists, your renderings became very valuable."

Jonathan put the cup of tea down on the end table near him, and started to chuckle. Soon, he exploded into deep, rich, infectious laughter, at the expense of his throbbing head. He held on to the bandage as he continued to laugh.

Kate was drawn into his merriment, forgetting the tension of the odd situation. She started to chuckle, not having the faintest idea what they were laughing about. "What's so funny?" she asked between giggles.

"I am obviously not dead. I always knew my work would be sold, but I do not recall being paid anything of consequence for them. For that matter, I was never paid anything at all!"

Kate shook her head. "Well, forgive me for sounding like a history professor, but you disappeared on July 17, 1868, never to be seen again. There were many rumors as to where you went, but most of them ended the same way. You were dead. Nothing makes an artist's work more valuable than death, I'm afraid. Even in today's world."

Jonathan's laughter faltered. "What is the date today, then?"

"It's...oh, my god, it's July 17th."

Kate stood, walked into the galley kitchen and leaned her hands on the counter.

They stared at each other in silence.

Jonathan looked away, back to his painting. He picked up the crumpet and took a bite, chewing slowly as he tried to get a grasp of the situation.

His thoughts wandered back to the days he worked on this piece. He and Margaret had taken to having daily picnics on the shores of Burrard Inlet. She would read her favourite books while he painted. She was his best critic and biggest fan.

They would feast on items she had carefully packed into the woven basket and make plans for their future. They would have children. Perhaps five or six. Margaret had already picked out several names.

He could see her beautiful, smiling face as clearly as if she were standing right in front of him. Her long, angelic blond hair braided gracefully back, exposing the creamy length of her slender neck. Her eyes, the color of sapphires, fairly danced as she laughed at his jokes. She was a delicate woman with soft, pure skin that he constantly ached to touch. Margaret always dressed to rival any of the wealthy aristocratic women of England. And she loved him. She loved Jonathan Edward Wilks. He was one of the luckiest men on earth to have her. He would do anything in his power to fulfill her every wish.

A sudden, ear-piercing noise erupted from the carriages racing past the building, bringing him back to the present. He turned to the window with a start.

"What in heaven's name is happening?" he asked, edging toward the window.

"It's called rush hour. Everyone rushes into the city every morning about this time, to go to jobs that most of them hate, to get pay checks that don't stretch as far as the month goes," she replied with a sigh. "Then in the evening, they all get in their cars and rush back out."

"What do you mean 'into the city'? From where?" he queried. "Where do they rush out to? And what is a car?"

"Jonathan, Gastown is only a very small district of a huge city now. Vancouver is the third largest city in Canada. The population of the city and its suburbs is over two million now."

Jonathan was about to ask another question when the front door opened, chimes ringing as a young woman entered the gallery.

"Hey, Kate! Sorry I'm late," the woman said, struggling with an armful of packages. She looked up and noticed Jonathan standing near the window.

Kate signed inwardly. *Here we go.* She would have to keep up the same story she told the paramedics. It seemed the most plausible, for now.

She stepped away from the kitchen, summoning up a cheerful smile on her face and, hopefully, in her voice. "Morning, Jenny! Were those idiots trying to run you down out there?" she asked.

"Almost. I swear, it gets crazier every day down here," she replied.

"You don't know the half of it," Kate said quietly. She noticed the inquiring look on her assistant's face and decided to jump right in. "Jen, I'd like you to meet my cousin, Jonathan. He just arrived from England."

Jenny Stephens smiled at Jonathan. "Hi, nice to meet you. Katie never mentioned that she had company coming."

Kate extracted some of the packages Jenny held. "Well, my Aunt Margaret had written me that he was coming, but I guess with all the confusion around here it slipped my mind. Jonathan, this is my trusty assistant Jenny Stephens."

Jonathan watched the exchange between the two women, deciding that he had better play along with Kate's fib. He bowed his head toward Jenny, and smiled brightly.

"The pleasure is mine, madam."

Jenny smiled at Kate. "Ooh, a proper Englishman. I just love to hear that flowing accent." She looked over at Jonathan, a frown appearing on her face. "What happened to you?" she said, noticing the bandage on his head.

Jonathan looked at Kate, completely at a loss for words. "Well, I was..."

Kate quickly jumped to his rescue. "He met the wrong welcoming committee on his way down here. Somebody mugged him."

Jenny's frown deepened. "Oh, you poor man! Are you all right?" she asked with obvious concern.

Jonathan smiled weakly. "Just a little bump on the head, but I'm afraid someone stole my bag..."

Kate interrupted again. "Yes, can you believe it? All of his travelers cheques, clothes, everything." She shook her head and laughed.

Jenny and Jonathan looked at her questioningly. She stopped laughing abruptly, and stammered, "Well, of course it's not funny. I just meant that it's a crazy welcome to Canada." Continuing the lie, she said, "I'm really sorry I didn't know you were arriving today, or I would have picked you up at the airport."

"Airport?" Jonathan asked, his brows furrowed in further confusion.

Kate tried to change the subject quickly. She was running out of fabricated lines. Turning to Jenny, she said, "We were just having a cup of tea. Would you like one?"

The look Jenny gave her was unsettling. Did she suspect something wasn't quite right?

"Sure. I could use a caffeine blast." She walked to the kitchen area and poured herself a cup of tea. Pointing to the packages she had dropped on the sofa on her way by, Jenny said, "Those are the mats you ordered from Sutter's. Oh, and I got some office supplies too."

Jonathan decided the best course of action was to just sit down and let Kate handle this sticky situation. He had almost given himself away already, and did not want to have to explain his predicament. Not that he could, even if given the opportunity.

While the women chatted, he looked around the gallery. Even though he knew now that he was indeed in the Hollister Rooming House, he did not feel at all at home. Well, of course he was not at home! He wasn't even in 1868! The entire situation was absurd. The question was, what was he going to do about it?

Then again, a part of his past still existed. His paintings. Something to connect him to the world he knew. But was he to stay here? He looked over at Kate, deep in conversation with her assistant. His heart ached for Margaret. Kate looked so similar to her that it was almost as if he was seeing Margaret standing before him. But she was not.

Kate was indeed a beautiful woman. Jonathan suddenly felt an uncomfortable sense of guilt, as he realized how good it had felt to be so close to Kate as she had helped him into the lounge. Her delicate hand had been warm against his shirt as she had steadied him.

How could he betray his beloved Margaret on this, their wedding day, with thoughts of another woman?

But their wedding day had never come. The wave of sadness that washed over him was almost unbearable.

Jonathan looked out the window again. What had become of this world? So many people. Dressed strangely. Vehicles constantly moving by, faster than anything he could imagine. Was he destined, even doomed to live out his days in such a furor of activity?

Shaking off the gloomy thoughts, he had to admit that this whole situation was rather intriguing. What other changes had occurred? Kate had said there were two million people in this city. What had she called it? Vancouver?

Jonathan vaguely recalled Margaret explaining the origins of the area. She had attended one of the finest schools in Canada, and was fascinated with historical subjects. She had explained that a British explorer by the name of Captain George Vancouver discovered the region in the late 1700's. History was something that he had never had much interest in during his school years.

But then, nothing about school had interested him. Which was precisely why his frustrated father had shipped him off, embarrassed that his youngest son took no interest in anything but, as he put it, 'useless endeavors in painting'.

But how could so many people now exist in such a small area of land? It was a day's journey to the nearest village. If he was supposed to stay here, in this time, he would have much to learn.

Jonathan was so deep in his own thoughts he did not hear Jenny speaking to him until she joined him on the sofa.

"I'm sorry. I was thinking about Mar...that is, I was trying to figure out a few things," he said, smiling at her.

"So how long are you here for?" she asked brightly.

Jonathan glanced at Kate, who seemed to be urging him not to say anything to give himself away. "I'm not sure," he replied, truthfully. "I'm just going to see what happens next."

"Well, too bad you've had such a dismal start to your vacation," she said sympathetically, looking at his bandaged head.

"Yes, well that was unfortunate, but I'm sure there are many interesting days to come," he said, smiling at Kate. "Wouldn't you say Kate? I'm so looking forward to discovering all that this wonderful city has to offer."

Kate cringed. He seemed to be enjoying this predicament. Jenny believed her hasty story so far, but how long could she keep up the charade? What on earth was she going to do with her 'visitor'? If he was going to be here for a while, she would have to hide him. She had enough on her plate as it was without having to keep up this lie to everyone he came in contact with. But then again, what other choice did she have but to lie? She could see it now. *Yes, everyone, this man is one hundred and fifty years old. He was supposed to marry my great, great, great grandmother, but something went wrong, and, well, he's here now. How do you like him so far?*

Her apartment would have to do for the moment. He certainly couldn't stay at the gallery. But what would she do with him all day while she was here? This was getting more complicated by the minute.

"I guess we'd better go back to my place and get you settled, Jonathan," Kate said cheerily, having made her decision.

Jonathan looked puzzled. "Your place? Don't you live here at the...the gallery?"

"No, although it seems like it sometimes. I have an apartment, a flat to you, about ten minutes from here. I have two bedrooms so you're welcome to stay as long as you want," she added, wondering, perhaps hoping that this waking nightmare would not go on for long.

"Kate's got a great place in Kitsilano with a fabulous view. You'll love it, Jonathan," Jenny said. "Only a block from the beach."

Jonathan smiled. "Well, I do love to spend time by the shore. I found I did my best work there," he replied, thinking back fondly to the sun filled days with Margaret.

"Work? What do you do, I mean that can be done on a beach?"

Jenny asked.

Kate and Jonathan looked at each other quickly, both searching for the correct fib to tell. "Actually Jonathan is an artist," she said.

Jenny smiled brightly at Jonathan. "Oh, really? I guess it must run in the family. You'll have to do something for us while you're here. We have any supplies you might need, don't we Katie?"

Kate was getting a tension headache. Slowly, she rubbed her right temple. "Sure. Anything he wants." It was time to make her escape. She finished the last swallow of her tea, taking her cup to the sink. "Let me just clean up a bit and we'll get out of here. I'm sure you're tired after your long trip, Jonathan."

He smiled at her knowingly.

She liked his smile. Kate felt that strange twinge again. Almost as if she really did know him. Perhaps it was because of the romantic stories she had heard from her grandmother and great grandmother. The photo of Jonathan and Margaret had always hung on their wall, reminding each woman who inherited it of the great love that once was.

Now that Kate had the photo, she too hoped that someday she would find that special man. Her one and only attempt at marriage had ended in divorce two years ago.

She and Allen had a dream of renovating the gallery and sharing the joy of showing and selling quality work from local artists. But that wasn't enough to satisfy him. His own agenda put him into debt way over his head. The fighting over finances got worse and worse, and finally Allen walked out of her life.

Now Kate was left to take care of not only her condo, but the burden of renovating and running the gallery on her own. The bankers were getting impatient. She was on the verge of losing the last tie to her family, and she didn't know what she could do to stop it.

While Kate cleaned the tiny kitchen, Jenny showed Jonathan some of the art on the walls of the gallery. He seemed to be genuinely interested, and Jenny was more than happy to go into lengthy descriptions of the pieces and their artists.

Kate could see why Grandmother Margaret had been so taken with him. As a little girl, Kate had looked at the heirloom photo often— Jonathan's handsome face, shoulder length, black hair, his straight postured stance. Back then he seemed like a prince. She dreamed that someday she would marry a man like him.

Now he stood just ten feet away from her, as real and more attractive than any man she had ever met.

Jenny walked to the sofa to pick up the bags of office supplies.

"I'll just put these away, Kate, then you two can be on your way. It shouldn't be too busy today, so don't worry about rushing back," she offered as she headed toward the back office.

"Thanks, Jen. You're a peach," Kate replied. Now she had to sort out her next step with Jonathan Edward Wilks. As long as she could keep him away from as many people as she could, for now, she might have a chance at surviving this situation.

Kate's state of relief was short lived. As she stepped away from the kitchen, she noticed Jenny coming out of the office—in one hand the photo of Jonathan and Margaret, in the other hand, the two halves of the coin.

Chapter 3

KATE STOOD anxiously as Jenny slowly walked toward Jonathan and stopped about ten feet away. He looked at Kate for direction, but she felt frozen, unable to help at all.

Jenny continued to scrutinize Jonathan from head to toe, looking from the photograph to him, and back to the photograph again.

Maybe she would just think it was some kind of coincidence, or family resemblance. They were not so lucky.

"You even have the same shoes on," Jenny said breathlessly, echoing Kate's earlier conclusion. "You're Jonathan *Wilks!*"

Kate's mouth went dry as Jenny looked to her for confirmation. Her heart was pounding. Should she tell the truth? What other explanation could she come up with? But would Jenny be able to keep such an unbelievable truth to herself?

Kate took a deep breath. At this point she felt further lies would only complicate matters, and she trusted Jenny.

"Jen, I don't quite know how to say this but..."

Jenny's look of confusion broke into an ear-to-ear grin. "You *are* Jonathan Wilks! Oh my god! This is so fabulous!"

Kate and Jonathan looked at each other again. Now *they* were confused. Jenny was certainly taking this better than they had.

Then Kate remembered that Jenny's interest in the world of metaphysics was quite strong. She had been trying to get Kate to go across the street for a reading from Clarice for years.

Jenny was still grinning. She turned to Jonathan and held up the two half pendants. "This is the other half, isn't it, the one that you gave to Margaret as an engagement present. Kate told me all about her necklace." She took a long breath, still smiling. "How on earth did you get here?"

Kate jumped in first. "We haven't exactly figured that out yet, but Jenny, you can't tell a soul about this! I know you believe in all of this stuff, but we just can't tell anyone, and I mean *anyone*! Okay?"

Jenny looked at Kate and frowned. "Yeah, you're probably right." Her smile returned quickly as she turned back to Jonathan. "But this is so cool! So really, how did you get here? Like some kind of time portal or something?"

"Let's sit down and we'll explain the only parts we know so far,"

Kate replied.

Jenny listened intently as Jonathan and Kate took turns explaining the events of the morning, both in his time and after he arrived at the back door of the gallery. Even with Jenny's input, they were no closer to a reason for his sudden appearance.

But Jenny discovered a major flaw in their contrived story. "You will have a problem if you try to pass him off as your cousin, though."

Kate frowned. "Why?"

Jenny sat back against the sofa and crossed her arms. "Because Jonathan never married Margaret. Therefore, you two have no related ancestors."

Kate looked at Jonathan, shaking her head. "That's right. Great. Just great. Now how am I going to explain your arrival?"

"Well, other than me, who knows he's even here?" Jenny asked, leaning forward again.

"Nobody, except for the paramedics," Kate replied.

Jenny smiled. "Then there's no problem! So what if they put his name down on their call report. It will just get lost in the bureaucratic pile, you'll probably never see those two again, and voilà! Nobody will ever know his real name. Be creative!"

Jonathan was puzzled. "At what should we be creative, madam?"

"Your new name, of course! How about Jonathan Buckingham, as in Buckingham Palace. That's quite British, wouldn't you say?" Jenny said, laughing as she faked an English accent.

Kate rolled her eyes, trying to suppress a smile.

"I have no intention, madam, of changing my name. The Wilks family has been well established in noble circles for over one hundred years, and I shall not tarnish our good name by participating in such a ridiculous folly," Jonathan responded indignantly.

Kate turned to Jonathan, somewhat surprised by his outburst. "Have you got a better idea?"

"Well...no. But I simply will *not* be known as Jonathan *Buckingham*!"

"Why don't you take him over to the Teahouse Café for lunch. Maybe Clarice could figure this all out," Jenny offered.

Kate shook her head. "No. I'm going to take him back to my place and keep him there for the moment. Maybe he'll just pop back to 1868 soon and we won't have to worry. No offense Jonathan," she added quickly. "We can't let anyone else find out about this, or they'd lock us up."

Jenny agreed. "Okay. You two get going. I'll take care of business today. Oh, here you go," she said, handing them back their respective necklaces. She looked at Jonathan and smiled. "I don't have a clue either why you're here, but it's a thrill to meet you. Your paintings are fabulous, and the story about you and Margaret is so wonderful. We should all be so lucky to find a guy like you, right Katie?"

Kate laughed. "Sure, but maybe one that is a little younger than one hundred and sixty!"

Jonathan scowled at her. "I'll have you know that I celebrated my thirty second birthday on May 14 just past. I would prefer you not deem me to be any older."

Kate continued to laugh. "I see men back then were just as worried about getting older as they are now. Some things never change. Come on, Jonathan. I have to get you into hiding."

The short ride to Kate's apartment was an adventure unto itself. Jonathan was petrified, and totally in awe at the same time. He spouted questions so fast that Kate never quite finished answering one before he was asking another.

How did they build such tall structures? Where were all the horses? Where was that man's voice and the music coming from? Why had they cut down all of the trees? Why was everyone in such a hurry?

As they drove past the park at Kitsilano Beach, Jonathan commented with disdain, "All of those men and women are practically naked! Have you people no sense of decency and decorum at all anymore?"

Kate slowed to a stop for a red light and followed his gaze. She chuckled softly.

"You may have a point. But these people are on the beach. They're wearing normal beach clothing. Don't worry. I'm sure you'll get used to it."

Jonathan seemed to have fixed his attention on two particularly well-shaped women in their early twenties. They were playing Frisbee in very teeny bikinis. Yes, it wouldn't take him long at all to adjust.

Kate slid her Toyota Camry into a spot near the front door of her apartment. "Well, here we are. Home, sweet home. At least until we figure out what to do with you."

Jonathan got out of the car and surveyed the neighborhood, a cluster of low buildings. He shook his head in disbelief as he looked from one corner to the next.

He turned to see Kate reaching into the back of her vehicle to retrieve a piece of art. Jonathan couldn't help but stare at her shapely body, noticing the snug fit of her dungarees as she bent forward. His body tightened in response.

A man came out of Kate's building, and gave Jonathan a thorough once-over as he passed. Kate grasped Jonathan by the elbow and guided him to her apartment.

"Come on, we have to get you out of public view," she said as she ushered him through the front door.

Once inside her apartment, Kate relaxed. She put on the kettle and opened the sliding balcony door. A mixture of ocean breeze and summer scents rushed into the stuffy room. She gave Jonathan a quick tour of her apartment and showed him to his bedroom.

"Let me have that heavy coat. You must be just roasting in those wool clothes. We'll have to do something about that.

He discarded the calf length suede coat and handed it to her. Kate was drawn to the movement of his tanned, muscular forearms as he rolled up the long sleeves of his white cotton shirt. Again, she wondered what it would be like to be held by those arms.

She had to stop reacting like this! She had been single too long, she decided.

"I'll try to explain everything later. All you need to know now are the basics—light switches, locks, and plugging in the kettle for tea," Kate said as she placed two teabags in antique teapot. She was too tired from working all night restoring his painting to be the ultimate hostess.

Jonathan had not said much since he had come into her home. "I am very sorry to inconvenience you this way. I cannot even pay you for my lodgings."

Kate took the freshly brewed tea and two mugs out to the spacious deck and set them on the table under a bright yellow and blue umbrella. She sat in the shaded side and motioned Jonathan to join her.

"Don't worry about it. I'm sure we can work something out. In the meantime, sit down and relax. You may be here for a while, so you might as well get used to it," Kate replied as she poured the tea.

He didn't answer, or sit down. Kate turned and found him standing at the railing, facing the scenic knot of buildings in the downtown core of Vancouver. What was to her a beautiful panoramic view of the North Shore Mountains, beyond the cluster of buildings, must be somewhat disconcerting to Jonathan. His world had been so different. Her heart went out to him.

He finally joined her at the table, sipping slowly on his tea and glancing often at the downtown skyline. Kate pointed out several areas of interest. Interesting to her usual tourist guests anyway, hoping to make Jonathan feel more at ease.

Kate found it fascinating to be able to discuss mutually familiar locations around Gastown with him, even though there was over one hundred and thirty-five years difference between the times they had both walked through the doors of the buildings. They were still no closer, however, to coming up with a reason for his appearance in her time.

Jonathan seemed to be having some difficulty keeping his eyes open. Kate took his empty cup into the kitchen and suggested he take a bath and go to bed. She would have let him use the shower, but it would be best to keep the bandage on his head dry for at least another day.

Kate ran the water deep in the oval, Jacuzzi tub in her *en suite*, and laid out fresh towels. She ushered Jonathan into the bathroom and told him that as soon as he was settled in the tub, he should push the button on the wall for a surprise. So maybe she was having some fun at his expense. She was sure he wouldn't mind the end result.

She had somewhat expected the shouting. Jonathan bolting from the bathroom, a towel barely covering his manhood, was something she definitely hadn't counted on. Kate didn't know whether to laugh or to... well, she didn't quite know what to do.

A wave of attraction hit her like nothing she had ever experienced before. She could barely breathe. He stood before her, dripping all over the floor, raving about the tub water beginning to boil, and all Kate wanted to do was touch him. To feel the strength of his legs under her exploring hands. He was a beautiful man. Tall, muscular, and masculine.

"Are you listening to me, madam?" he shouted. "I said..."

"Jonathan, I'm sorry," Kate replied, coming out of her libidinous stupor. What had gotten into her? "It's called a Jacuzzi. It wasn't fair of me to trick you like that. If you don't like it, just push the button on the wall again and it will turn off. It's supposed to help your muscles relax. Try it. You'll like it once you get used to it. I promise."

Suddenly remembering the state of undress he was in, Jonathan quickly retreated into the bathroom and slammed the door.

"I'm sorry," he called from the other side of the closed door. "I hope I didn't offend you. I should have put my clothing on before I, uh, that is..."

Kate laughed. He was either a nineteenth century prude or very shy. Either way, she liked that quality.

"Look, Jonathan, just get back in the tub and *relax!* I've got to go to the market and get a few groceries. You might want to get some sleep. I'll pick up some summer clothes for you while I'm out," Kate said, grabbing her purse and heading for the door. "I'll be back in an hour or so. Just make yourself at home."

Kate slid behind the wheel of her car, but hesitated in starting it. She stared ahead, remembering the sight of Jonathan standing nearly naked in front of her. The sensation that she knew him returned. She was drawn to him, physically and mentally. So strongly that she felt overwhelmed.

As if she didn't have enough to consume her life already. Kate started the car and pulled out into the quiet side street. She had thirty days to come up with ten thousand dollars, or the gallery would belong to the bank, not that it didn't already, with the heavy debt for renovations.

Jonathan's painting she was restoring would probably bring in about eight thousand, and she had the Bateman that was promised to Mrs. Tonquest—another two thousand. But that would only bring her up to date with the bank. What about next month? And the month after?

Business had been slow lately. This was usually the best time of the year for Kate, being tourist season. Bus loads of tourists flocked to Gastown, but this was the year of Native carvings, something Kate had been meaning to get into selling, but had not as yet. Things would pick up, she told herself. They had to.

Particularly since she seemed to have another mouth to feed. Jonathan Wilks. Under her very roof. It really was a shame that she had to sell one of his last...

She had Jonathan Wilks under her roof! Jonathan Wilks, whose paintings went for thousands of dollars!

No. The idea was ludicrous.

One of the main reasons that his paintings sold for so much was because they were antiques, painted by a man who was dead. No. She shelved the idea immediately.

She had to do everything she could to keep Jonathan out of sight until he either went back to where he came from, or she came up with a brilliant explanation as to why he was here.

Kate arrived at Granville Island Market, thankful that there were plenty of parking spaces in the usually overflowing lot. She would get all of her shopping done as soon as she could and get home. No telling what twenty-first century dangers were lurking in her apartment to a man who had never even seen a ball point pen! *Electricity, for one,* she thought.

Forty minutes later she was done. As she placed the bags of fresh fruits, vegetables, breads and other market specialties in the trunk of her car, she spied a sports clothes shop across the cobblestone boulevard. Jonathan had to have something else to wear. She closed the trunk and went into the store.

The shop sold strictly casual wear for both men and women, fortunately at bargain prices. Perfect for Kate's current limited budget. The sizing was simple—Small, Medium, Large, XL. Jonathan's muscular body came easily to mind. Shaking off the images that once again flooded her mind, Kate decided Large would be the safest, and picked out a couple of T-shirts, shorts and pull on nylon track pants with a matching jacket.

This was not something she could afford right now. She hoped her credit card wouldn't be rejected.

As Kate left the shop, she heard someone call her name. She turned to see Spencer Thomas, editor of the weekly Kitsilano Courier, walking toward her.

"Hey, Kate! What brings you down here so early on a weekday?" he asked with a bright smile, slipping his hands into the pockets of his gray twill walking shorts.

"Unexpected visitors and an empty fridge," Kate replied. "How are you, Spence?"

"Just great! Really looking forward to the gallery opening next weekend. You will be there, won't you?" he asked.

Kate stared at him blankly. "Gallery opening?"

Spencer gave her a look of surprise, and laughed. "Don't tell me you've forgotten? Your star prodigy, remember? Monica Foster? Her grand opening?"

Kate gasped. Monica had worked at Kate's gallery for three years, and had always dreamed of owning her own shop. Kate had helped to guide Monica to her dream, and had promised to be there opening night to celebrate, and lend moral support.

Now, with Jonathan around, she was going to have to review her entire calendar. She didn't want to leave him on his own any more than she could help.

"Sorry, I've had a lot on my mind lately. And having company kind of puts a crimp in things. I'll have to do some juggling," Kate replied.

"So bring your visitor along. The more the merrier. You know how mundane these things can be, the same old crowd every time. It might be nice to get some fresh faces in the room," he urged. "And I'm sure Monica would like to see as many people there as possible."

As many people as possible. All the more reason to keep Jonathan as far away from there as she could, Kate thought.

"I'll have to see what his schedule is. He just arrived," Kate said.

"Okay, it's your call, but I'm sure he'd be welcome. Gotta go. We've got some holes to fill for this issue. See you later," he said with a wave as he walked toward the market.

Kate returned to her apartment, fumbling with the many bags from her shopping trip. She didn't hear anything as she entered her suite.

"Jonathan?" she called out softly. Maybe he was asleep. She dropped the groceries on the kitchen counter and, taking the bag of clothes, walked down the hallway to the spare bedroom. The door to the spare room was ajar, so she pushed on it lightly, calling his name gently.

He was asleep, lying on his stomach with one arm above his head. He looked peaceful, the lines of tension from his ordeal erased, leaving a softness to his handsome face. The sheet covered only his lower body, revealing his muscular back. Kate breathed a long sigh.

Was it just the outer package that Margaret had fallen so deeply in love with? Or was the man beneath just as beautiful? Why had Margaret gone against her father's wishes and almost married this man?

Kate took the clothes out of the bag and laid them on a chair near the bed. She tiptoed out of the room and quietly closed the door.

After putting the groceries away, she went into her own room and collapsed on the bed. It had been a very long night. She had about three more hours of work to restore Jonathan's painting to the point where she could sell it.

It was the last thing she wanted to do, especially now. How could she sell something that belonged to Jonathan? Would he be upset that she was selling something that connected him to the only existence he knew?

She had no choice. The bankers wanted their money, and she didn't have any sale pending that would come close to what she could receive for Jonathan's painting. There were several buyers who were interested in his work. She would just have to make him understand what was at stake. Her heritage. His former home. There really was no other option.

Kate stared at the ceiling until she felt her eyelids becoming heavy. Maybe if she just had a nap, she would have more energy to deal with her problems. She felt her body sinking into the softness of the mattress. She gave into the pull of deep sleep.

KATE OPENED her eyes and looked around. Birds chirped in a nearby tree. Pure white, fluffy clouds floated through a perfect azure sky. A creek gurgled behind her.

"Well, what do you think?" asked a familiar voice.

She turned to see Jonathan putting the finishing strokes on a painting, the antique easel it sat on balanced in a field of tall grass. She recognized it as the painting she'd had to sell only two weeks ago.

Jonathan's shirt sleeves were rolled up. He wore the same pants as when he arrived at her back door. He looked happy, and there was no sign of the bandage on his head.

Kate smiled. "That was one of my favourites. It sold last week for six thousand dollars. I really hated to let it go."

Jonathan laughed. "Margaret, my dear sweet woman. Perhaps you've been in the sun too long. You're not making any sense."

Kate was confused. Why was he calling her Margaret?

Jonathan put his brush and palette down and walked over to Kate. Taking her by the hand, he suggested they go back over to the river and finish their picnic.

Kate stumbled as she walked through the tall grass. Looking down, she noticed she was wearing a long, full, cotton dress.

They sat down on a bleached white Hudson Bay blanket near the bank of the river. Jonathan stretched out on it, resting on one arm. He reached into a large picnic basket and pulled out some bread, breaking off a piece and offering it to Kate.

As she nibbled on the fresh, homemade bread, Jonathan just stared at her, a look of complete love shining in his eyes. He reached up and gently lifted the half coin necklace from the bodice of her dress. The brush of his fingers against her chest sent a chill of wanting through her. Their eyes locked, and Kate felt as if she was under a spell. A spell of love greater than she had ever known.

"I don't care what your father thinks," Jonathan said as he let go of the necklace. "We will build a life together. Our children will be brought into a home filled with love that they will never doubt." He took her hand and slowly lifted it to his mouth, brushing his lips softly against her fingers, one at a time.

Kate was overcome with desire. This couldn't be happening. She wanted him to touch her, to feel his lips against hers.

Jonathan sat up for a moment, then moving closer to her, he slowly leaned into her, until she was lying on her back, their eyes still locked. Kate could feel the dry grass against her hair as Jonathan bent his head and softly kissed her neck. It was like a low voltage shock wave running through her. Her entire body tingled.

Jonathan placed his hand on her stomach, his lips tracing the length of her neck. She felt his hand move, further up her abdomen. His hand lightly brushed the swell of her breast and....

KATE WOKE UP with a start. Her heart hammered wildly, and she felt hot. Flushed with desire.

She sat up and looked around the familiar surroundings of her bedroom, trying to shake off the vivid dream. Even her breathing was rapid. She took a few cleansing, calming breaths and fell back against her pillows.

Something poked at her ear. She reached up to move it away, then

quickly jumped off her bed, shaken by what she found.
It was a long piece of dry grass.

Chapter 4

THE DRY GRASS fluttered to the carpeted floor of Kate's bedroom. She stared at it as if she had never seen the likes of it before.

"This can't possibly be happening," she whispered. But twelve hours ago she wouldn't have believed that she would have a time traveler sleeping in her guest room. Her world was turning upside down.

Kate paced the room, repeatedly looking at the inanimate piece of grass lying at her feet. A low chuckle escaped from her lips. *And you thought the problems with the bank would be rough!*

She needed a calming cup of tea. As she headed down the hall to the kitchen, she heard muttering from the guest room. Jonathan must have woken up, but who was he talking to?

She knocked lightly on the door, and called his name. Jonathan opened the door fully. Kate was pleased to see that he was wearing the track pants and T-shirt she had purchased. He looked good. Too good. But the expression on his face was not a happy one.

"Is something wrong?" she asked. Perhaps the clothes didn't fit as well as they looked.

"I certainly hope that these are not the only pieces of clothing you purchased," he said with a tone of disgust.

Kate crossed her arms, insulted by his comment. "I didn't have a lot of time, nor did I know what size you were, so yes, these are the only clothes I bought. What's wrong with them?"

Jonathan snorted. "You can't possibly expect me to be seen in public like this! These are nothing more than under garments, save this," he said, picking up the matching nylon jacket.

Kate was still tired, she was still trying to adjust to the whole situation, and she was broke. How dare he chastise her for doing him a favor in spending her hard earned money!

"Look, I don't want you to be seen too often in public at all! And if you are going to be around for any length of time, you can't be wandering around in the clothes you arrived in," she replied forcefully. "I'll get you some other clothes later, but for now this will have to do. They are perfectly acceptable summer clothes, so just live with it!"

Kate turned and stomped down the hall to the living room. She clicked on the television, needing some sort of modern day distraction to calm her nerves. Continuing into the kitchen, she plugged in the kettle then turned to the serene mountain view outside her kitchen window.

She thought of the piece of grass. Where had it come from? And the dream. The dream had been so real!

Lost in her thoughts, she didn't hear Jonathan come into the living room. The heavy thud as he slumped on to the leather sofa in front of the television brought her around.

Kate turned to see Jonathan staring at the television, a rerun of *Roseanne* keeping his attention. She walked into the room and sat down beside him. He never took his eyes off the screen.

"It's called television," she said, not sure how he would react to yet another common aspect of the new century he'd been thrown into.

"Why are those people so small?" he asked, a sense of awe in his voice.

Kate laughed. "It is just an image of them that is sent to the screen by...well, I don't know how exactly, but everybody has one in their home. It's how we get information about what's going on in the world." She picked up the remote control and flipped through several channels, settling on the local noon newscast.

"Almost anything you want to know about the world is here," she said, waving the remote control. "Right at your fingertips. Just press here, where it says channel," she said, handing him the device.

Jonathan took it warily, and as Kate had done, pointed it at the television and pushed the button she had indicated. The picture changed, and Jonathan broke into a short laugh. He did it again, and his laughter grew.

"My Lord, this is absolutely amazing!" he said, still laughing and continuing to press the button.

"Great," Kate muttered. "He's already got the hang of channel surfing. He's a man, all right." Instead of tea, Kate decided she needed a brisk shower to make her feel better.

"Jonathan, I'm going to jump in the shower, so help yourself to anything in the kitchen. I won't be long." He didn't answer, his eyes glued to the changing images on the screen. "Never mind," she said, as she headed to her bedroom.

Twenty minutes later Kate felt better, more refreshed. She changed into shorts and a tank top and returned to the living room. Jonathan was still in front of the television, but he had stopped surfing. He had found the news channel again, and was watching intently.

Kate watched as the news anchor described a brutal murder that had taken place last night in a downtown bar. She heard Jonathan gasp, and turned his way. He was no longer watching the news, but was staring at her, his gaze roaming from head to toe and back.

"Madam, must you? I know things are different now, but a lady should not parade around half naked, even in her own home. I really must protest," he said defiantly, although his gaze was still taking in every inch of her.

"Jonathan, this is a different world than you're used to, so I'm sure there will be a lot of things you'll have to adjust to. But I am not going to change my lifestyle for you. Now, if you're up to it, why don't we go down to the beach for a walk and get some fresh air. I'm sure we could both use some," she said, hunting through the hall closet for her runners.

She brought them back to the living room and sat down to put them on. Then it occurred to her that the one piece of apparel she hadn't thought about for Jonathan was shoes. Kate closed her eyes and sighed. More money. She really couldn't afford this. They would have to improvise, she decided. He would have to wear his boots to walk two blocks up to the nearby Wal-Mart then they could drop off his old ones on their way back.

Soon they were strolling slowly along the sidewalks that meandered through the park at Kitsilano Beach. Jonathan was once again amazed at the modern 'level of undress', although he was not doing so in a complaining fashion as he had at her apartment.

After stopping to buy burgers and fries at a beach side concession stand, they wound their way through the throngs of sun worshippers to find an empty spot by a large log.

Jonathan commented on all of the children running around them on the beach and playing in the water. "This seems to be very much a family area."

"Yes and no. Kitsilano is mostly an area for single people and young couples, but as you can see by the packed parking lot, everyone comes here."

"If I may be so bold, how is it that you have never had any children? I mean, a beautiful woman of your...that is to say, I would have taken you to be married and taking care of a man and his family."

Kate laughed. "You were about to say a woman of my age? I'm only thirty-one. I know that in your day most women would have been married for at least ten years by now, and probably have at least five children, but I still have plenty of time. My career comes first at the moment."

She avoided his gaze as she continued. "Besides. I was married, and we did plan to have children, but that's all over now."

Jonathan detected sadness in her voice. Quietly, he asked, "Did your husband meet an untimely death?"

"No, unfortunately, he's still around. I thought he would just go away, find someone else to sponge off of, but he pops up once in a while just to make my life miserable."

"How so?" Jonathan asked, then changed his mind. "Forgive me. It really is none of my business."

Kate turned to him and smiled. "It's okay. You may as well know the truth, just in case he surfaces one day." She reached for her drink and took a long swallow.

"His name is Allen Brigham. We were married almost eight years ago. I had no idea at the time he was into gambling. I found out soon after our wedding, though, and he kept promising me he would stop. He did for a while, but then went back at it. After we got the loan to renovate the gallery, it seemed to get worse. Maybe it was my fault. Maybe I spent too much time working and not enough time paying attention to him."

She stopped for a moment, noticing Jonathan's intense concentration on what she was saying. This was probably more than he should, or wanted to hear.

"Go on," he encouraged, taking a bite of his burger.

Kate sighed, and continued. "He got in over his head. He was supposed to make the payments on the mortgage and I would handle the payments on the renovation loan. He never had any money, and I managed to cover for him for a while, but I wasn't making enough at the gallery yet to handle it all. We fought constantly, and one night he just left. We were divorced two years ago. And now, just to top it all off, the bank is about to foreclose on the gallery if I don't come up with a lot of money, very soon."

"Are you saying that..."

"Yes, Jonathan. I could lose my family's home. Your former home for that matter."

Jonathan didn't know what to say. His life of nobility had always surrounded him with people of immense wealth and displayed dignity. Divorce and loss of fortune were not something that, if occurring, was ever discussed openly.

"So you never had any children with this man?" he asked.

"No. We had planned to, once we got the gallery going, but..." Kate's voice trailed off, her throat constricting with the pain of remembering a life of promises unfulfilled.

She had wanted to have children. She had waited to get married until she had finished art school, and thought she had laid her life out perfectly. She married a handsome, up-and-coming attorney. They had a great circle of friends, a wonderful place to live and lived the good life. Somewhere along the line, something went wrong.

Kate took a deep breath, and changed the subject, needing to break away from the memories. "Anyway, now you know. Let's just relax and enjoy this beautiful day."

Jonathan took his cue, and began to ask her more questions about his new surroundings.

Kate continued to answer him as best she could. Although interesting, Kate found it disturbing that he had so much to learn. If he was destined to stay, how would he be able to function in her world? She couldn't keep him holed up for long, but it would be very risky to let him come in contact with too many people. She decided to approach the subject and see if they could come up with a solution together.

"Jonathan, if you are going to be here for a while, we have to come up with a story about your background. Since we can't pass you off as my cousin, we have to be very careful when you are around other people. No one can know the truth."

Jonathan knew she was right. He put his burger down and silently stared at the water. Although he was loathe to admit it, he was somewhat afraid of the consequences should he give his real identity away.

But then again, he was a man of refinement. All his life he had been schooled in proper etiquette. Not that he had always used it, which was precisely the reason his family had shipped him off to the new world in the first place. But given any social situation, he had been able to hold himself with the grace and diplomacy bred to his long line of English aristocracy. He was sure he could do the same now, with a few minor adjustments, of course. He would just have to be careful.

"Fear not, my dear Kate. I will do my best not to give away our little secret," he said, finally, giving her his best smile.

Her return smile melted his heart. He felt himself being drawn to her more with every passing hour.

"I have to tell you about a dream I had earlier," Kate said. "It was very strange. I was in a field, and you were there, putting the finishing touches on a painting that I sold two weeks ago, and—"

Jonathan gasped and she stopped speaking, her stare telling him she was aware of his disconcertion.

"What's wrong," she asked.

He spoke slowly. "And then we walked to where we had a blanket laid down by the river, and finished our picnic."

Kate looked ill. "How did...I mean, that was my dream! How could you possibly know what I was dreaming about?"

He continued to look directly into her eyes. "I don't, but I had the same dream, except it wasn't just a dream. Margaret and I did have that picnic, and that is where I painted that piece. But in my dream, I felt I was with Margaret, but instead, it was your face. When I awoke, I thought it was a result of my situation, and that my thoughts were jumbled, but if you had the dream too, then I am at a complete loss."

Kate didn't know what to say, what to do. She felt like she was being drawn into a world where she did not belong, a world that belonged to two people from the past. What else was going to happen? This whole situation had gone from unbelievable, to bizarre, to frightening. What was the purpose of all this?

"Something isn't right. It's like we've been connected for a purpose, but nobody is giving us any clues to the puzzle," Kate said, thinking out loud. She played with her pendant absently.

Jonathan noticed what she was doing, and reached out to touch the gift he had given to Margaret with such love. "Maybe the coin has something to do with it." His fingers brushed the softness of her neck as he gently took the half coin from her hand. Her skin was every bit as soft as Margaret's. He felt the briefest shiver from Kate.

"Maybe this is the connection that brought us together." He sighed heavily as he let go of the pendant, and looked out toward the water. "There has to be a reason."

"Kate? Kate, it is you!" A woman's voice from behind startled them both from their thoughts. A slim, blond woman in her thirties hopped over the log they were sitting behind and sat down beside Kate.

"Lisa, what are you doing down here in the middle of the day?" Kate said brightly.

"Playing hooky. I can't stand to be cooped up in that office tower on a day like today," the woman replied, not sounding guilty at all for taking time off work. She turned her attention to Jonathan and extended her hand. "Hi. I'm Lisa."

"Oh, sorry, Lisa. This is my friend, Jonathan," Kate said hastily. Another test. Just what she needed.

Jonathan jumped into his role immediately. He took Lisa's hand and leaned forward to kiss the back of it briefly.

"I'm pleased to make your acquaintance, Lisa," he said, turning on his accent.

"Oh!" Lisa said, blushing as Jonathan kissed her hand. "Such a gentleman. Where are you from?"

"England, actually. I've only just arrived," he said, smiling mischievously at Kate.

"What part of England are you from? I have some relatives in

Liverpool," Lisa continued, not waiting for Jonathan to reply to her question.

Jonathan glanced at Kate briefly. "I've lived in various parts so I don't have any particular place that I call home. However, I did spend a lot of time in a very small town called Worchester."

Lisa beamed. "Oh, how romantic! I'd just love to see some of those quaint small English towns."

Kate groaned inwardly. Lisa was an acquaintance from Kate's previous job, before she started the gallery. She had not particularly spent any time with Lisa, but now she was acting as if they were old friends. She was flirting very obviously with Jonathan, and he was lapping up every minute of it.

She listened as Jonathan asked Lisa questions about herself, effectively steering her away from talking about his own background. And from Kate. Lisa seemed to have forgotten she was even there, totally enraptured with Jonathan. Her twittering, false laugh was getting on Kate's nerves.

Jonathan gave Kate a look that seemed to say, "See, you have nothing to worry about."

Maybe she was overreacting. It was, after all, a seemingly safe environment for Jonathan to try his hand at socializing in the modern world.

Lisa did most of the talking, thankfully, and most of her questions seemed to be directed to what Jonathan wanted to see while he was here. She suggested several places he might like to see. He nodded politely, telling her that he would have to add them to his list of 'appointments'.

Kate thought he might be in trouble when Lisa asked him how his flight was. He glanced over to her briefly with an unspoken request for help, and she jumped in.

"Oh, you know how those transcontinental flights are, Lisa. Ten hours of bad food, movies you've probably already seen, and sleeping, if you're lucky," Kate interjected.

Parroting her, Jonathan quickly took his cue. "Indeed. If you are lucky. Quite uneventful, really," he added, belying the fact that he had no idea what they were talking about.

After another fifteen minutes, which Kate had to admit went quite well, Lisa finally seemed ready to leave. It seemed they had passed the first real test of Jonathan's ability to handle his new century. Kate began to relax, but it didn't last long.

"So, are you going to bring Jonathan to Monica's gallery opening next weekend, Kate?" Lisa asked hopefully. She was looking at Jonathan as she posed the question to Kate.

Kate tried to look and sound nonchalant. "We haven't had a chance to discuss it yet. Jonathan only arrived this morning," she replied, again seeing that Lisa was not paying any attention to her, totally infatuated with Jonathan. Small pangs of jealousy surfaced and Kate felt uneasy.

Unaware of her discomfort, Jonathan smiled broadly at Lisa. "A gallery opening? What a splendid opportunity! I'd be positively delighted to attend." He quickly turned to Kate. "If that's all right, with you, my dear Kate."

Before she could answer, the air was filled again with Lisa's twittering laugh. "Oh, I just *love* the way you talk, Jonathan. Wouldn't it be nice if some of the men around here had manners like that, Kate?"

Lisa's laugh bubbled over again, and Kate smiled back politely. "Yes, wouldn't it though," she replied through her false smile. She wished Lisa would just go.

"Kate, you have to bring Jonathan along next weekend. I'm sure he'd love it," Lisa continued. "There will be all kinds of people there and I'm sure they'd love to meet him."

Jonathan must have read the look on Kate's face. "We'll have to see what next weekend brings, Lisa," he answered, speaking for both of them. "It sounds very tempting, however. I shall endeavor to make time to attend."

Lisa seemed content to leave it at that, and stood to leave. "Great! Well then, maybe I'll see you there, or maybe at the beach sometime again. Nice to meet you, Jonathan." As an afterthought, Lisa turned to Kate as she walked away. "Catch you later, Kate."

Kate waved her good-bye, and watched Lisa for a moment as she wandered slowly along the boardwalk bordering the beach. When she turned back to Jonathan, he seemed to be looking at her curiously.

"What."

Jonathan smiled slowly. "If I didn't know better, Miss Carston, I would say that you are acting somewhat jealous."

Kate glared back with as much indignation as she could muster. She couldn't let him know that he was right. She didn't believe it herself, but she was. Full blown, green-eyed jealous.

Why?

She didn't even know Jonathan. But the feelings were there none the less. Feelings that seemed to belong to someone other than herself. Like in the dream.

Jonathan had said he had dreamed about the day he and Margaret had gone to the riverbank for a picnic, but it was Kate's face he had seen.

"Jonathan, the dream I had, that is, we had. How could that have possibly happened?" Kate asked, needing to get some distance from the emotions that were developing in her.

"Yes, that is quite odd. I have never experienced anything of the like, nor have I even heard of it." He laughed softly. "But then again, anyone who would dare to mention something so ridiculous would surely have been locked away as a madman."

Kate agreed. "People of today are a little more open-minded to the unexplainable, but I'm not one of them. Or at least I wasn't. Obviously I'm going to have to rethink my opinion."

Kate picked up a handful of sand, let it slowly fall out of her hand, then repeated the gesture, creating little piles between her feet. She was very aware of Jonathan beside her. She wished he would speak. She wished she could. But neither did.

Chapter 5

FROM BEHIND them on the boardwalk, a woman's voice called out. "Jonathan, you come back here right now! Jonathan? Jonathan, where are you?"

Kate whirled to see a woman clearly in search of a child, but the words triggered a memory. A voice. A woman's voice calling out the name Jonathan. Somewhere in her past she had heard it. But when? Where?

Her thoughts took her to the attic of the gallery, but at the time she was five years old.

The child Kate took the old hairbrush set out of one trunk, a shawl out of another, and sat in front of the mirror at the vanity table on the burgundy, velvet-covered stool, pretending she was a princess.

It came through almost like a whisper, only a bit louder. "Jonathan, where are you? Jonathan? I can't find you!"

The woman on the boardwalk called out again, jerking Kate back to the present to find her Jonathan staring at her strangely. She shook off the memories.

As a child, she never did learn whose voice it was, and when she asked her mother if someone had been downstairs calling for a man named Jonathan, her mother and grandmother had just laughed. "No Katie, you must have imagined it," her mother said.

Then her mother turned to her grandmother and added, "Maybe she heard Margaret. Maybe she's up there somewhere, still looking for Jonathan Wilks." They laughed, and Kate's mother patted her on the head and sent her outside to play. Kate never mentioned it further, but she did hear the voice again.

As Kate grew up and spent less and less time in the building, she forgot about the voice. Until now. The woman on the boardwalk calling for her son brought back the memory. Kate remembered it as clearly as if she had heard it yesterday.

Excitedly, Kate turned to Jonathan. "She was in the attic!"

Jonathan was taken aback by her outburst. He had no idea what she was talking about. "Who?"

"Margaret! I heard her calling your name when I was a child. I used to play in the attic. I played dress up with all of the old things in the trunks. I used to hear a woman's voice calling for 'Jonathan'."

Jonathan was confused. "Why didn't you say anything about this before?"

"Because I haven't thought about it for years. It was a long time ago. My mother and grandmother told me I was just hearing things. But she was there, Jonathan! Margaret was in the attic with me!"

Jonathan didn't say anything. What was there to say? He didn't believe in ghosts any more than Kate did, but here they both were. Thrown together into a situation that was mad. Absolutely mad. And it seemed more and more in the direction of something to do with his beloved Margaret.

Was she still with him in a spirit form? Would he be with her again soon? The thought filled his heart with hope. If just once more, he could hold his precious Margaret in his arms, and tell her that he would do anything within his power to keep the promise he had made to her. That they would never be apart once they eloped.

At the same time, the thought that Margaret might be so close to him, and yet so unreachable, made him sad. Why had he been dealt such a cruel hand? What was he to do?

Kate was standing up, preparing to leave. Jonathan wasn't sure his legs would carry him any distance. He felt somewhat dizzy. Surely it was just the confusion of the circumstances. He stood slowly, and silently helped Kate gather the empty wrappers and paper cups from their meal.

"Something is happening to both of us, Jonathan," Kate said softly. "Maybe she is trying to get some kind of message to us."

He nodded in agreement. "Maybe she has been trying for years, but you were the only one she could get through to."

Kate wandered over to the caged wastebasket and motioned for Jonathan to throw the wrappers in. "But why now? I have enough on my plate already, without having to turn into Nancy Drew and solve a ghostly mystery."

"Nancy who?"

Kate sighed. "Never mind. I just mean that if I don't come up with a way to get the bankers off my back, everything my family worked for will probably go to some foreign investor, who will tear down the gallery and put in a modern glass and marble monstrosity. All in the name of progress and profit."

She turned to Jonathan, and steeled her shoulders against the imaginary foes of the future. "I won't let them do it, Jonathan. I will not let them take the gallery away from me!"

Jonathan joined in her determination. He was beginning to feel he would play some part in helping her realize her goals.

"Right then!" he said confidently. "We shall do everything in our power to save your gallery. What will we do first?" he asked enthusiastically.

Kate turned and stared toward the cluster of downtown towers, beyond which was her humble gallery. Her determination wavered slightly, but she took a deep breath. She could do it, but how?

The woman she had heard earlier was chasing after her son again. Kate watched as the woman ran ahead of a little brown haired boy and held out her arms. She laughed as her son ran gleefully into her grasp. "I got you, Jonathan!" She hugged her son tightly.

Kate felt her body tingle. She knew she would receive help in her quest. Margaret had sent Jonathan to her. It was becoming clearer with every moment.

She turned to Jonathan. He was also watching the woman and her son.

With a heavy heart, Margaret watched Jonathan and Kate walk up the boardwalk. She missed him so very much. If only she could touch him again, to feel his strong arms holding her tight. But she had a mission to complete. It was important for everyone's sake that she ensure the outcome would be as it should. Still, her love for Jonathan Edward Wilks had not dimmed in over one hundred and forty years. It would be eternal.

Margaret breathed a lonely sigh as she began to follow her true love and her beloved descendant back to Kate's home. Kate really did have a flair for decorating. Just as her mother and her grandmother did. She had done wonders to the Gastown house as well. Such a pity she couldn't just live there.

Margaret smiled as she continued following Kate and Jonathan. There were so many wonderful memories in the Hollister Rooming House. She recalled the first time she had seen Jonathan, or rather didn't see him, until it was too late.

"OOOF!" MARGARET blurted as she stumbled back into the foyer. "I'm terribly sorry, I should have been watching where I was—"

Her gaze locked with eyes so blue they were mesmerizing. Like a foolish schoolgirl, she merely stared. He was the most handsome man she had ever seen. He seemed to be staring right back at her.

"Ah, you must be Mr. Wilks." Margaret's father's booming voice rang out behind her. "Margaret, dear, don't just stare at the man. He is a guest for heaven's sake. Where are your manners?" James Hollister stepped past his daughter to take one of the many suitcases from his new customer, and with a hearty slap on the back said, "Welcome! Welcome to the Hollister Rooming House. I'm sure you'll be very happy here! Your family made an excellent choice in arrangements for you. And may I say, welcome to Gastown. It's a growing community, and I'm sure with your fine breeding, you will be a welcome addition to the town."

Margaret felt her face flush with embarrassment. Not only for the way she had acted, but for her father's obvious over exuberance towards this man, even though she had heard him utter disparaging remarks about the 'cast off remittance man'.

Jonathan Wilks. He was a remittance man. She had read of the like, but had never actually met one. He didn't look any different, although she didn't know what exactly she would have expected a remittance man to look like.

Certainly not this handsome. His clothing was made of the finest wool. Margaret noticed that each piece was tailored perfectly to his body.

Why would anyone of such obvious refinement be banished from his home? Be sent clear across the ocean to a little town that did not even have so much as a proper theater? Surely he would miss the fine culture that was so abundant in England.

Someday she would go to England, Margaret mused. She would travel the world. Meet interesting people. Maybe even stand on the doorstep of so many of the wonderful buildings she had read about in her books. Maybe even meet the man she would marry.

James Hollister continued to ramble on to his newest, and presumed wealthy guest as if Margaret wasn't even there. She stood quietly at the bottom of the stairwell, holding on to the polished wood ball on the railing. She couldn't take her eyes off him. It was as if some great force had taken the breath from her.

He looked back at her often as her father spoke. Each time, she felt little butterflies rise in flight in her stomach. He was a magnificent man.

As Margaret's father prepared to take him upstairs to his room, she moved to the parlor, sat on the large brocade chair by the fire, and picked up her needlepoint, trying to be as inconspicuous as possible. It was also a good vantage point to watch the newcomer.

He continued to stare at her as he mounted the stairs. For the life of her, Margaret could not look away from his eyes. Why did he affect her so?

Before long, Mr. Wilks came downstairs again. He had changed into cooler clothing, and was no longer wearing his hat. His hair was clean and shiny. It was longer than most of the men in Gastown wore theirs, which made him look even more worldly, like he truly was from a land far away.

He smiled as he came into the parlor and sat on the sofa adjacent to Margaret. "I'm afraid I haven't had the pleasure of your acquaintance yet, madam. Allow me to introduce myself. I am Jonathan Wilks."

Margaret extended her hand daintily. "A pleasure to meet you, Mr. Wilks. My name is Margaret Hollister."

Jonathan took her hand and gently kissed the smooth skin in true gentleman fashion. Margaret felt a tingling that went straight up her arm, and seemingly to her heart. It seems an eternity before he let go of her hand.

She tried to concentrate on her needlepoint as she spoke, fighting the urge to continue gazing into the endless depths of his eyes. "How long will you be with us, Mr. Wilks?" she asked. She could tell he was still watching her closely.

"I'm not certain. It was not my intention to come here in the first place, therefore I'm not quite sure how long I shall have to stay. However, I dare say that I have already seen one thing I think will make my stay here much more pleasant than I had anticipated," he ended, his voice softening.

Margaret glanced up, and was once again drawn into his eyes. It was as if something beyond her was connecting them. She had never felt this way about any man she had only just met.

"I was wondering, Miss Hollister, that is, if you are not previously engaged, if you might show me some of the sights?" he asked.

"I would be happy to, Mr. Wilks." Margaret put her stitching down and stood. "Although I'm sure there is nothing very interesting here in Gastown, compared to the architecture of England. But we do have some sights you might enjoy."

As Margaret spoke, her father entered the room again. She looked at him, waiting. He gave a slight nod, indicating he would approve of her showing Mr. Wilks around Gastown. Margaret turned back to Mr. Wilks and smiled.

She felt her knees almost give way as he smiled back at her. He had dimples, which gave him a youthful, almost boyish look, yet he was every bit a man.

Margaret could feel people stare as she and Mr. Wilks strolled along the boardwalk through the main street. She pointed out the general store, the livery, the collection of saloons and other rooming houses or hotels. He took it all in, seeming very interested.

She felt his presence strongly as he walked beside her. No man had ever made her feel like this. She wondered if he was feeling the same toward her?

OVER THE next few weeks, Margaret and Jonathan became constant companions. He would catch her eye at the dinner table, and it was as if they had a secret language no one else could see or hear. She was falling in love, much to the chagrin of her father, who had begun to make up chores for her to do every time she mentioned any plans with Jonathan.

They managed to spend a lot of time together, despite the growing annoyance of her father. Margaret took great pride in packing Jonathan's favourite foods in a basket so they could sneak away for an entire day. She learned he was an artist, and was indeed very talented. He had ordered several pots of paint and rolls of canvas from Mr. Harrison at the general store, and assured Margaret that some day his renderings would be worth a great sum of money. Every home in Gastown would proudly display his work.

Margaret pretended to read her books as Jonathan painted, but as often as she dared, she would just watch him. She loved the way his brows furrowed as he concentrated on his work. With his shirtsleeves rolled up, she could see the muscles in his forearms moving as his hands magically transformed the blank canvas into a beautiful work of art.

None of the people in town liked Jonathan's paintings, but Margaret knew it was his passion, and she loved every stroke of the brush he labored over.

He hummed as he painted. An endearing quality, Margaret thought. Often he would stop, look over at her and smile. That was all it took. She was falling deeper in love with him every day.

It was getting harder to find excuses to see him alone. Margaret's father had mentioned his dissatisfaction in her spending so much time with Jonathan, but he was not so bold as to insult his wealthy guest by forbidding him to see Margaret. Margaret often had to change their plans as her father came up with yet another chore for her to do, just as she was about to go on an outing with Jonathan.

Soon, though, her father would have no choice in the matter. Margaret lay in her bed watching the sun rise on another beautiful day. Last night, Jonathan had given her his heart, and a beautiful engagement present. Margaret ran her fingers gently over the jagged edge of the half coin on the delicate chain. It was the most precious gift she had ever received, because Jonathan wore the other half of the coin. She knew that wherever they were, they would not be complete without each other, just as the coin would always be two halves of something whole.

Margaret did feel whole when she was with Jonathan. She remembered one of his early comments, while they were picnicing on the shores of the inlet a couple of weeks after his arrival. He had said, with sadness, that he didn't feel quite like he belonged anywhere. Not in England, not by his family, yet he didn't feel like he belonged here in Gastown either.

Margaret wrapped both hands around the half of the coin she now wore. "You belong here, Jonathan Edward Wilks," she said softly. "You belong with me." She closed her eyes and smiled. They were going to elope, and they would be together for the rest of their lives. She had never felt so happy.

A LOUD CRASH startled Margaret away from her memories. Two men were unloading a large piece of glass from a truck and it had slipped, splintering on the pavement. They were both blaming each other, yelling obscenities as if no women and children were present. Margaret saw Kate pulling Jonathan away from the foray, telling him not to get involved.

Margaret watched the scene unfold and shook her head. This lifetime was very difficult to understand. She was almost glad she didn't actually have to participate in it on a daily basis.

But she had her work to do as well. And in some ways, it may be a more challenging task than anything the people of this age had to handle.

THE DAYS leading up to Monica's gallery opening passed without incident. Jonathan seemed to be settling into the modern world, not unlike a tourist on an extended vacation to a foreign land. Kate had finally begun to relax about Jonathan's existence in her life. She was still no closer to figuring out why he was here, but she had tried to get on with her life at hand, and let things happen as they would.

She hadn't managed to find a good enough excuse to keep him away from the gallery opening in two days, however. She still wasn't comfortable with the idea of letting him loose on unsuspecting Vancouverites.

The other day, while listening to one of her newer clients discuss the ambiance of old Gastown, Jonathan had asked the woman if she was aware of the fact that Gassy Jack wore two pair of under shorts because he chafed easily.

Kate wasn't sure if it was true or if he was just pulling their legs, but regardless, it was a little piece of trivia that didn't need to be shared. She worried about what other 'interesting' quips about the past he would come up with, at the wrong time or to the wrong people. All he needed was to run into one of the local historians, and he could risk exposing his real identity.

Earlier in the week, Jonathan had asked Kate if he could set up his own area in one of the upstairs rooms to paint. He had told her that he needed something to take his mind off the current predicament he found himself in, and he could only go to so many tourist outlets in any one day. Kate had agreed, thinking it would be an easy way to keep him out of the way.

As the days passed, Jonathan found himself spending more and more time in his private working area. He listened to the comings and goings of daily business of the gallery, but kept to himself. He had been desperately trying to come up with a plan to help Kate with her financial problems, but he did not know enough about this world to conceive a really solid idea.

On the day of the gallery opening, Jonathan was putting the finishing touches on a painting, when an older woman, dressed in the very finest of summer wool dress, walked into his work area. Startled, he turned and smiled at the her.

She seemed somewhat embarrassed, and started to back out of the room. "Oh, I'm sorry, young man. I was looking for the powder room. I didn't mean to interrupt you," she said apologetically.

Jonathan just smiled in return. "Not to worry. It's the next door on the left."

The woman turned again to go, then stopped, noticing the detail Jonathan was adding to his painting. She stood in the doorway for a moment, then slowly edged toward him.

He stopped his work, and looked at the woman. She was standing behind him, tapping one finger against her right cheek. Jonathan felt uneasy. Even though Kate had said that his early works had sold for quite a tidy profit, Jonathan was steadying himself for the familiar jeering that he had heard so regularly the men in early Gastown.

After several moments, the woman spoke. "This work is extraordinary, young man," she said, clasping her hands together and smiling. "Has this piece been commissioned by anyone in particular?"

Jonathan was surprised by her admiration of his work. "Well, I, uh, no, it has not. Thank you for your kind words, madam."

The woman took a few steps back and looked at the quiet waterfront scene Jonathan had created. She silently took it in from several different angles. "Yes, this is just what I've been looking for. What did you say your name was?"

Jonathan stood and extended his hand, then noticing he had several streaks of color on his fingers, pulled back and reached for a cloth, quickly wiping the excess paint off. He stepped forward again, and extended his hand, introducing himself with a renewed sense of pride.

"Allow me to introduce myself, madam. My name is Jonathan Wi..." he stopped abruptly, forgetting their new routine for a moment. "Jonathan. I am a friend of Miss Carston's. I'm visiting here from England." In the past few days, he had begun to feel confident that he could follow through with the charade of his newfound life. He couldn't afford any slip-ups now.

The woman took his extended hand daintily and smiled broadly. "Very nice to meet you, Jonathan. I would like to purchase this painting."

Chapter 6

JONATHAN WAS at a loss. He had taken note of the exorbitant prices that most of the paintings were selling for in Kate's gallery, but he had no idea what to sell his for, or whether he should sell it at all. He could already hear Kate's concern about exposing his identity to the public. However, he had done exceedingly well so far, and this would be a way to help pay his way while he was here. Yes, surely she would have no objection to him selling some of his work.

But he would not take on the responsibility without first consulting her. This was her gallery, and her time. Jonathan smiled politely to the woman, and gently ushered her back into the hallway.

"I'm afraid you will have to consult Miss Carston about purchasing anything in the gallery, including my modest work, although I sincerely appreciate your offer, madam."

"Yes, I see your point." Seemingly forgetting the destination that brought her upstairs, the woman called over the balcony to Kate.

"Kate, dear! Oh, Kate, I really must talk to you about the fabulous discovery I've made up here!" she said, pulling Jonathan toward the railing.

Kate finished her conversation with another customer and looked up. Her heart leapt to her throat as she saw her best customer, Mrs. Sumner, standing at the railing with Jonathan at her side. She couldn't quite read the look on Jonathan's face, but she knew something was up. What fabulous discovery had Mrs. Sumner been referring to? Kate wasn't sure she wanted to find out.

Taking a deep breath, Kate put on her best business like smile. "What kind of discovery, Mrs. Sumner?"

"My dear, you've been harboring an imported treasure up here! A veritable treasure!" Mrs. Sumner bubbled. "I must have this young man's latest piece! It's exactly what I've been looking for!"

Kate was not expecting this. She had seen the piece Jonathan was working on, and it was as good, if not better than any of his works she had at home or in the gallery. What if someone recognized the similarities? She had tried so hard to keep him away from the public. This was not something she had counted on, nor wanted to deal with at the moment.

Jonathan noticed the look of impending doom cloud Kate's features.

He turned to Mrs. Sumner, and suggested she return to the lounge area while he discussed the sale of his work with Kate. She agreed, but seemed determined to buy his work.

Kate smiled at Mrs. Sumner as she reached the main floor of the gallery. "Please help yourself to some tea and pastries, Mrs. Sumner. I'll have to speak to Jonathan about this privately for a moment." Kate smiled as she grabbed Jonathan's arm and pulled him toward the back office.

Once inside, Kate tried to keep calm as she closed the door. "Jonathan, we have to have a little chat," she said, motioning him to take a seat on the sofa. She paced the small room for a moment, then turned to Jonathan.

"What in God's name do you think you're doing?" she said angrily, standing in front of him, her hands clenched at her sides. "This is exactly the type of thing I wanted to avoid! How am I going to explain this? If Mrs. Sumner buys one of your paintings, it won't be long before someone in the local art world sees the similarities between that one and the one hundred and forty year old originals!"

Kate began to pace again, not waiting for Jonathan to get his opinion in. "Similarities? What am I thinking! The only differences will be the quality of paint you are using now." She stopped pacing and stood directly in front of Jonathan again. Kate noticed that he was merely sitting back and smiling up at her. Smiling! Was he nuts? Didn't he realize the gravity of the situation?

Jonathan patted the sofa beside him, and spoke quietly. "Come, my dear Kate. Sit. Can't you see what a perfect opportunity this is?" Kate made no move to sit, so Jonathan stood, placed his hands on her shoulders, and gently guided her to sit on the sofa. He sat beside her and took one of her hands in his.

For a brief moment, they sat quietly together, neither saying a word. But Jonathan felt comfortable. Something was happening to him, a kind of settling calm growing within. As if he belonged here, in this time, with this woman. She needed him, and now he had a way to help her.

"If this Mrs. Sumner would like to buy my painting," he began softly, "then why not sell it to her? I have already explained that I am a friend visiting from England, and there is no reason for her to believe otherwise. It would be a way for me to help you with your debt to the bank. And, of course to help repay you for the large sums of money you have already put out, due to my untimely arrival."

Kate sighed, torn between what was right, and the desperate financial situation she was in. Having earlier dismissed the very notion of selling any more of Jonathan's works, she felt herself bending to this new

Colors of Time 57

idea.

But it was wrong. And dangerous. The pretense of his existence was working so far, but this would be too much of a risk.

Yet it also seemed to be a short-term solution to the problem. Maybe she could let Jonathan sell some paintings for his own spending money. At this point, she simply could not afford to pay for his living expenses as well as her own.

Kate relented, her shoulders dropping in resignation. "But what if someone did question the similarities?" she asked, still holding on to his hand. It felt good to be this close to him.

Jonathan thought for a long moment, then smiled at Kate. "How does this sound? I've come over to Canada to follow in my long lost relative's footsteps. That being the long since dead Jonathan Wilks. He came to Canada to make his fortune over one hundred years ago. Perhaps we can say that I too am on a journey to find myself!"

"Find yourself?" Kate started to laugh. "Find yourself? You've been watching Oprah again, haven't you." Kate's laughter grew. "Besides, you didn't come here to make your fortune. Your father shipped you off to get you out of his hair, as I understand it." This situation was getting more ridiculous by the day. But now it was comical.

"Jonathan, you simply can't sell that painting to Mrs. Sumner. I realize that you want to help, but I don't know that this is the way. We can't risk exposing your identity."

Jonathan realized he was still holding her hand, and with her growing unease, her grip was tightening around his fingers. He had to think of a way to take care of this situation.

"Right, then. Here is what we shall do." Reluctantly letting go of Kate's hand, Jonathan stood and began his own slow pacing of the tiny office. "I will not sell my painting to Mrs. Sumner at this time. I shall tell her that if she would like to buy it, or any other of my pieces at a future date, I would consider it. But right now, I am just starting to develop my collection, and I would like to refrain from selling any until I can get just the right piece for her."

He stopped pacing as he finished relating his idea and stood in front of Kate, smiling down at her, satisfied with his resolve of the situation.

Kate was not completely impressed. She stood, tilting her head back to look him squarely in the eyes. "And what would that solve, except delaying the inevitable. Mrs. Sumner usually gets what Mrs. Sumner wants. Since she's my best customer, she would probably be suspicious if I was the one who poured cold water on this idea."

Jonathan shrugged. "But it is not you, my dear Kate, it is I who am not willing to sell my painting. Let's just put it down to...what was that phrase I heard Mrs. Potter use the other day? Ah, yes. Artistic temperament. I am going to have an artistic temperament."

Kate shook her head and laughed. "Jonathan, I think you ought to just—"

A sharp knock came at the office door. Jenny poked her head inside and smiled apologetically. "Sorry to interrupt, but Mrs. Sumner is starting to get a little over-anxious out here. Have you made a decision?"

Kate sighed. "Tell her we'll be right out."

Jonathan took Kate by both hands and brought her around to face him. Kate felt the familiar glow of being with him rise from her hands to her entire body. Every time he touched her, whether in passing, or like this now—intentional, comforting—she felt it. A connection. As if he had been a part of her life for a very long time. For a moment neither of them spoke, both lost in the feeling that surrounded them.

Finally, Jonathan broke the silence. "Please understand, dear Kate, that I will find a way to help you with your debts. I have but one resource at the moment, my painting. Maybe if Mrs. Sumner is willing to buy one of my works, my current works, I can sell more. Please," he said softly, "let me do this for you."

Jonathan bent his head slowly, and brushed his lips tenderly against Kate's cheek. He stood straight again, feeling a rush of emotion toward her. She was very special, very important to him, even though it had been only days since they met. Her eyes seemed to be searching his for an answer as to what was happening between them. She shook away the moment, pulled away from his grasp, and headed out of the office. Jonathan breathed a heavy sigh, and followed her back to the gallery lounge.

Mrs. Sumner clasped her hands together and smiled brightly as Kate and Jonathan came into the room.

"Tell me, then. What is the price of that beautiful painting, young man?" she said enthusiastically.

Kate looked briefly at Jonathan. "Jonathan's decided, Mrs. Sumner, that he is not ready to sell his work at this time."

"Oh, no!" Mrs. Sumner said with over played anguish. "Young man, I simply must have that painting!"

Jonathan stepped forward, smiled, and took Mrs. Sumner's hand. He bent forward and placed a gentleman's kiss on the back of it. As he straightened he said, "Then, Mrs. Sumner, you shall have it, but I must ask that you wait for delivery until I can finish the others that I am going to put in my upcoming show."

Kate and Jenny stared at Jonathan, dumbfounded.

Mrs. Sumner tittered with delight. "Wonderful, wonderful! How exciting! A show of your own. Kate, why didn't you tell me about this intriguing young man earlier?"

Kate was finding it hard to breathe, much less answer her question. His upcoming show? He was digging himself, and Kate in deeper by the moment.

Jenny stood back, a smile slowly forming. Kate did not see the humour in the situation, and glared at Jenny, who quickly turned and walked into the galley, busying herself with cleaning up the afternoon tea dishes.

"Well, I, uh," she stammered, "I, that is we wanted to wait, as Jonathan pointed out, until he had more work to show." She resigned herself to the fact that one way or another, Mrs. Sumner was going to buy that painting. "Besides, we haven't settled on a selling price for that piece, and it wouldn't be fair to hold you up in your search for a piece for your living room."

Mrs. Sumner smiled, and clasped her hands together again. "Well then, I guess I'll have to help you along with that decision." She stood and walked over to where Jonathan and Kate stood. "I'll pay you two thousand dollars for that piece, Jonathan. Not a penny more, although I dare say that if your work is always this good, you and I will be having this discussion again in the near future."

Kate knew that his other works had sold for at least three times that amount. "Mrs. Sumner," she began, "we really have to—"

"Sold!" Jonathan shouted, grinning from ear to ear. "Mrs. Sumner, I hope you're happy with the first Jonathan Westham painting to be sold in Canada." Two thousand dollars! That was as much as he had won the entire evening at the Deighton Hotel. For one painting!

Kate was thrown yet another curve. Jonathan Westham? Where on earth had he come up with that name?

Mrs. Sumner was elated with the sale. "I'll be waiting anxiously to get that painting home, young man, so please let me know the second I can take it." She picked up her purse and headed for the front door. "Ta-ta everyone. This has been a wonderful surprise, Kate. You really must let me know when Jonathan's show will be. I'd be happy to spread the word about him."

Just as she reached the door, she turned and smiled at the group. "I do hope we'll see you tonight at Monica's opening, Jonathan."

Kate, Jenny and Jonathan waved silently as Mrs. Sumner breezed out the door. They turned and looked at each other, and Jenny's tightly controlled laughter burst out first. Jonathan looked at Kate and started to snicker nervously. She was not amused. She could just see what was coming tonight as Mrs. Sumner bragged about her 'new discovery' to everyone at the gallery opening.

She did feel somewhat relieved, though, that he had created this new identity. At least she wouldn't have to justify the second coming of Jonathan Wilks. Hopefully he wouldn't have to use this name where he would need proper identification, not that he had any. Still, he was not in her good books.

"Jonathan, I swear, you are going to get me into so much trouble! A show? The object of the exercise is to keep you away from the public, not to invite them in to this nightmare!" Kate said, trying to keep control of her frustration.

Jonathan gathered Kate into his arms. "My dear Kate, I would do nothing of the sort. I have not signed the piece I am working on yet, and as I said, Mrs. Sumner will have the first of many Jonathan Westham paintings. Surely this can't be a problem." He gave her a reassuring hug.

Jenny's laughter had subsided. "Kate, you have to admit that it is the ideal scenario. He's just an unknown guy from England, named Jonathan Westham. You know that Mrs. Sumner will be on the phone to all of her friends bragging about the fabulous new artist she 'discovered', and before long, there will be a lineup of wealthy women just clamoring to have one of his paintings. All he has to do is turn on that wonderful British charm and he'll have them eating out of his hands!"

Kate pulled away from Jonathan's embrace, threw her arms up in the air in resignation, and walked back to her office. "I give up!" she said, knowing she was outnumbered.

AS KATE finished getting ready for Monica's gallery opening, her stomach tightened with nervous anticipation. Taking Jonathan to this function was the last thing she wanted to do, but he had already been seen by too many people who were going to be there tonight. If he didn't show, she might end up spending half the night explaining his absence.

He had managed to handle himself, for the most part. As Kate stared at her reflection in her bedroom mirror, she silently said a little prayer to help her get through the next four or five hours. Please, just let us get there, mingle, and get home—in one piece!

She went into the living room, finding Jonathan in his now familiar position in front of the television. On one hand, he was using it to help him fit into this modern world, but he was also becoming a walking commercial. The other day he had a discussion with Jenny on the finer points of tartar control toothpaste.

Kate had to once again stretch the limit on her credit card to buy Jonathan something to wear tonight. Teaching him the proper technique with his tie had been an interesting exercise. But the end result had been worth it. He looked devastatingly handsome in the charcoal gray pleated pants and hunter green shirt. Her stomach fluttered as he turned and smiled up at her, patting the sofa beside him.

"I know you are somewhat apprehensive about this evening, but let me assure you, I am ready for this. I will exhibit exemplary manners befitting the occasion," Jonathan offered, smiling reassuringly.

Kate sighed as she sat down beside him, not quite convinced that they could pull it off.

"I have been to functions in the art world, you know. As a matter of fact, I often attended splendid gala evenings at some of the finest galleries in England. This shall be a walk with cake, as they say."

Kate frowned and shook her head. "That's 'cake walk', or 'a piece of cake', Jonathan. Don't go overboard trying to fit in. It will backfire, and then we'll both be in trouble."

She looked at her watch, then taking a deep breath, said, "Well, I guess it's show time. Come on. Let's get this over with."

Jonathan stood and extended his hand to help her up. "Have faith, my dear Kate. We may even find that this evening could be, dare I say, fun."

Kate gave him a sidelong glance as she reached for her purse. She didn't object when Jonathan held her hand as they left the condo.

The evening was well on its way by the time they arrived. Thirty or forty people were milling around the small, but elegant gallery. Tuxedoed waiters circled among the guests, offering glasses of champagne and colourful canapés.

"Kate! There you are!" said an elegantly dressed woman in her thirties. She walked quickly over to Kate and Jonathan, giving Kate a long hug. The woman turned to Jonathan.

"And this must be the famous Jonathan Westham. Mrs. Sumner has been telling everyone about you! Hi, I'm Monica."

Jonathan smiled and inclined his head. "The very same, madam. May I say it is a pleasure to finally meet you. I've been looking forward to your opening all week."

Monica turned to Kate. "My, he certainly is as charming as Mrs. Sumner made him out to be. Come on, you two, let me introduce you." She stepped between Kate and Jonathan, hooked her arms through theirs, and guided them into the throng of guests.

The evening was going smoothly, and Kate began to relax. Jonathan had been mingling for over two hours with most of the guests, having been enthusiastically introduced to almost all of them by either Monica or Mrs. Sumner. So far he had been the perfect gentleman. He asked people about either the works being exhibited, or themselves, steering them clear of talking about his background.

Kate saw one of her customers, and as they discussed a particularly unusual piece of sculpture, she glanced back to Jonathan. Her heart skipped a beat as she saw him in an earnest discussion with Spencer. Knowing that it wouldn't take too long for the investigative reporter in Spencer to emerge, Kate excused herself from her present conversation and crossed the room quickly.

"Ah, there you are," Spencer said brightly as Kate approached. "Your friend here has a very keen sense of the art world."

Kate's stomach lurched. What had they been talking about? How much, or what had Jonathan said? She had to get him away from Spencer.

"Yes, yes he does. Can I steal him away from you for a minute, Spence? There's someone I'd like Jonathan to meet."

Spencer smiled at Jonathan. "Sure, no problem. I think he's the hit of the party tonight." Looking around the room, he chuckled. "You may have to hose down a couple of the women before you can get him out of here tonight."

Spencer and Jonathan shared a man-to-man laugh at the joke. Kate managed a small laugh as she guided him to another part of the room, but she was not amused. The last thing she needed was to have one of the many single women here tonight get too close to Jonathan.

When Lisa arrived, she wasted no time zeroing in on Jonathan, but she had a lot of competition. From across the room, Kate realized every woman in the place seemed to be taken in by his English charm.

Kate felt someone nudge her from behind. Turning around to apologize for being in the way, she saw that she was alone. No one stood within six feet of her, but a strong scent of jasmine filled the air.

Thinking she had imagined the feeling, Kate turned her attention back to Jonathan and the group of women that surrounded him. She noticed that now Lisa had her arm linked with Jonathan's and was gazing up at him, taking in every word he said with the enraptured eyes of a schoolgirl in love.

This was ridiculous. She was not jealous. What possible reason could there be for that? Even if he did belong here, in this time, he almost married her ancestor!

The thought made her smile. But Lisa's grip on Jonathan's arm annoyed Kate to no end. Or was it the way that Jonathan seemed to be reveling in all of the attention from the women? Shouldn't they be taking in some of the art at Monica's grand opening? Instead of Jonathan?

Kate stumbled forward, toward the group. This time someone had definitely pushed her. She turned around quickly, but still found herself essentially alone in the corner of Monica's gallery. A waft of jasmine scent drifted past again.

Another memory from her childhood suddenly flashed by. Jasmine. Whenever she had played in the attic and had heard the woman's voice, Kate had smelled a strong perfume. At the time, she had just thought it was from the clothes she used to play dress-up. Where was the scent coming from now?

A woman's voice whispered urgently, "Go!"

Was Margaret with them? It couldn't be. Kate shuddered as she felt a warm breeze pass across her arm. This couldn't be happening!

Obeying an overwhelming urge to leave, she walked quickly to the throng of women around Jonathan, and tapped him on the arm. "Sorry, ladies, I've got to steal him away from you. I have an early day tomorrow, so we have to be going," she said, feigning an apologetic voice.

A chorus of ooh's and nooo's came from his new found fans, but Jonathan realized she was serious, and extracted himself from Lisa's amorous hold.

"Ladies, it has been a wonderful evening. I shall look forward to seeing you again soon," he said as he bowed slightly, generating tittering laughs from two of the more awestruck women.

Jonathan followed Kate to where Monica stood, discussing a particularly odd sculpture with Spencer. She was disappointed that Kate and Jonathan had to leave, but stepped forward to hug Kate warmly.

"You have no idea how much you have helped me, Kate. I couldn't have done this without you," Monica said. "And Jonathan, it was a pleasure to meet you. Let me know when I can put some of your pieces in my gallery. Don't let Kate hog them all!"

Kate hoped her shock wasn't too obvious. Somewhere in the evening she had missed that part of the conversation. Great. More exposure.

As they headed to the door, Spencer stepped forward and extended his right hand toward Jonathan. "Great to meet you, Jonathan. I'll drop by the gallery in a couple of days and take you out for that beer."

Jonathan shook his hand and replied, "Yes, quite. That sounds like a marvelous idea."

Great! Now he has a drinking buddy! Kate took Jonathan's arm, almost dragging him through the doorway. She had to get out of there. For both their sakes.

The short drive back to Kate's condo was strained with silence. Finally, Jonathan asked, "Are you not feeling well? Or is there some other reason you chose to make such a hasty exit from what seemed to be a splendid evening?"

Kate turned to look at Jonathan as she stopped for a red light. "She was there, Jonathan. She pushed me."

"To whom are you referring?"

"Margaret, of course!"

Jonathan laughed. "My dear Kate, even if my Margaret was somehow able to be in the room with us, why ever would she push you?" He laughed again, heartily.

"I don't know! But I'm telling you, something or someone pushed me. When you were in the middle of your fascinating conversation with that harem of women."

"Harem of women? I should hardly think that having a discussion about art with local patrons is something to get upset about, my dear. Was that not why we attended this evening?" he asked. "And surely you just thought someone pushed you."

Kate let out a long huff of frustration. "I'm telling you Jonathan, something is going on!"

He patted her hand reassuringly as it rested on the gearshift knob. "Don't worry, dear Kate. I shall try to cheer you up with some wonderful news."

Kate wasn't sure she wanted to hear it. He had been involved in extended conversations with almost everyone there tonight. No telling what kind of a hole he'd dug for them this time.

"If it involves anything that will get us in trouble, I don't want to hear it," Kate replied curtly.

"Not at all. Not at all. In fact, it will establish me further as Jonathan Westham. No one will ever make the connection to my true identity."

"What do you mean, establish you further? Jonathan, what have you done?"

Jonathan smiled broadly. "It is not I who have done anything...exactly," he finished sheepishly. Then sitting up straight in his seat he announced, "I have been offered a job!"

Chapter 7

"WHAT!" KATE fairly screamed as she braked hard and pulled over to the curb. As soon as the car came to a complete stop, she spun around to face Jonathan, stunned by his revelation.

"What do you mean you've been offered a job? With whom?" she demanded.

Jonathan started to laugh, a nervous gesture Kate had come to recognize when he was about to say something she probably didn't want to hear. "Well, it's really quite farcical, when you actually think about it. I mean—"

Kate balled her fists in front of her chest, and through clenched teeth said, "Jonathan, just spit it out! What...have...you...*done!*"

He took a deep breath, and smiled boldly. "Your friend Spencer, lovely chap that he is, has asked me if I would like to write a weekly newspaper column on art exhibitions happening in the Vancouver area."

Kate's mouth dropped open in awe. She tried to speak but no words formed.

Jonathan continued quickly. "Yes. Well, it seems he thinks that I have a rather unique outlook on art. We were discussing at length some of the pieces that were being displayed this evening, and—"

"I don't believe this," Kate said quietly, dropping her head to the top of the steering wheel. She sat for a moment, not saying a word.

Jonathan reached over and placed his hand on her shoulder. "Are...are you not feeling well?"

"Just shoot me now," Kate replied sarcastically. Looking up from the steering wheel, she gazed out the front window. "Somebody just shoot me now."

"My dear Kate, I rather see this as an opportunity, don't you?"

Kate turned to look at him. The excitement in his face was hard to miss. He obviously wanted to do this. But now he would not only be exposing himself to a few people in the immediate art world, he would be opening himself up to the entire city! Everyone who was anyone in the local art world read the *Courier*.

"Jonathan, we are just going to get ourselves into more trouble doing things like this."

Jonathan knew she was right, but he had to start living. Who could tell how long he was going to have to live his life in this time? If it was to be for any length, he wanted to be a part of it, not just hide in a corner room of the gallery. He wanted to contribute to Kate's life. To make her happy.

He had begun to realize just how much he cared for this woman. Maybe it was because of the obvious similarities to his Margaret, but she was also a gentle soul, as Margaret had been. Even their laugh was the same.

Jonathan somehow felt compelled to take care of Kate in the days, or even months, to come. Since she wouldn't let him sell his paintings, he had to find a way to help her with her financial problems. The one hundred dollars weekly that Spencer had offered him was a wonderful sum of money. All he had to do was attend a few showings, and write down the events of the evening, or afternoon as it were. How hard could that be?

And he would do it all under his new identity—*Jonathan Westham.* No one at the party tonight blinked an eye when he was introduced, or introduced himself under that name. No. There was nothing to worry about. He had found the answer.

Jonathan hesitated, but knowing in his heart that it was the right thing to do, he took a stand. "I am taking Mr. Thomas' offer, and I will not hear another word about it!"

"How about two words. 'Work—permit'."

She had his attention. He had been about to continue, but stopped, looking at Kate questioningly.

"You can't tell me that one has to have a permit to do an honest day's work in this country now," he replied, puzzled.

Kate pulled the car back on to the road. As she settled back into the flow of traffic, she began to explain the difficulties he faced.

"People can't just waltz into the country and do whatever they please. Anyone who isn't a citizen here, which you are not, has to have landed immigrant status, or a working visa, of which you have neither."

"Well then, I shall just have to get one. I shall make time to do that first thing in the morning."

Kate sighed. "Jonathan, surely even when you came to Canada in 1867 you must have had to have some type of papers to get into the country!"

"Well, no, I am a British subject and we require no papers, despite the fact that I was a...remittance man," he said, scrunching his face sourly as he said the word. "My Lord, the very word sickens me. But the fact is that I have never worked. No man in the Wilks family has ever had to work, in the traditional sense of course," he replied, proud of his heritage.

Kate shook her head. "Of course," she said dryly. "I forgot. You are a true blue blood. Unfortunately none of that counts at the moment. And even if you had some sort of legal identification now, it would take months before you were legally allowed to work here. Spencer can't just hire you and pay you. Unless he pays you under the table, and he is not about to risk his paper to do that."

"What do you mean risk his paper?"

"At the moment you are not here legally. Did he even ask you about whether or not you had a work permit?" Kate asked, turning on to her street.

Jonathan hesitated. "Well, not exactly. We were quite absorbed in topics of discussion pertaining to the pieces being shown. He thinks quite highly of you, too, I might add."

Kate smiled, in spite of the predicament they were in. Spencer was a good friend. She thought very highly of him also. Which was precisely why she didn't want to get him in any trouble by hiring Jonathan. She drove into her building's underground parking, trying to decide what course of action to take.

She pulled into her spot, turned off the engine, and looked at Jonathan. "I'm really sorry to burst your bubble, but this simply will not work. You'll just have to tell Spencer that you've changed your mind."

They walked up to Kate's apartment in silence. Once inside, Jonathan went into the living room and dropped heavily onto the sofa, not pursuing the subject any further. She didn't know whether that was an acceptance of her decision, or if he was thinking about other ways of convincing her. She didn't have to wait long for her answer.

As Kate poured them a glass of wine, Jonathan extended his arm across the back of the sofa and turned to her.

"There simply has to be a reasonable solution to this dilemma. I once knew a man in England who had arrived from Amsterdam without papers. He was some sort of criminal from what I gather, but he was a decent enough chap. Never bothered anyone. Always ready with a funny story. He wanted to stay in England, so he found a man who, through channels I know nothing about, obtained the required documents, and he lived a wonderful life in a small town just outside of Manchester."

Kate gave Jonathan a sidelong glance. "And your point is..."

Jonathan stood and paced back and forth in front of the sofa. "Well, my point is that there must be some avenue we could explore to do the same for me. Do you know anyone who might specialize in this sort of thing?"

Kate laughed. "No, Jonathan. Forgery is not one of my areas of interest. Nor is being sent to jail for being an accomplice. I'm afraid you're just going to have to accept the fact that you can't work for Spencer."

Jonathan sat down again as Kate came into the living room and handed him a glass of wine. He watched as she deposited her wine on the coffee table, and walked over to the stereo, pressing the play button on the CD player.

She was a beautiful woman, and lately Jonathan found himself studying her every move. So much like his Margaret, yet much more mature. Well, of course she was more mature. She was at least ten years older than Margaret had been when he last saw her. As much as he missed Margaret, he found himself being drawn deeply to Kate.

A part of him felt guilty. As if he was being unfaithful to Margaret. But she was gone. And Kate was right in front of him.

Kate was a strong woman who could hold her own in any situation. Jonathan had seen her talents as a businesswoman, as an extremely gifted art restoration expert, and she had even painted a few pieces by which he was most impressed. Even in the face of losing her gallery, her heritage, she had kept a stiff upper lip. Her strength and courage under such trying circumstances only made her more appealing. Jonathan was falling for her. And, it seemed, he was powerless to stop it.

Kate sat on the sofa beside Jonathan and patted his knee. "Don't worry about it tonight. If things are meant to be, something will happen. I'm a great believer in the—"

Kate stopped mid-sentence as the phone rang. She reached over to the coffee table and picked up the cordless receiver.

"Hello."

Jonathan took a sip of his wine and sat back against the colorful throw pillows in the corner of the sofa. He noticed that Kate had a scowl on her face. It seemed whomever was at the other end of the line was not someone she wanted to hear from. Even the tone of her voice had changed.

"I'm fine. You?" he heard her say.

She had picked up a pen on the coffee table and was drawing circles on the notepad meant for taking messages. She did not look at Jonathan. The stilted conversation continued, and Jonathan felt that it might be better if he left the room.

He took his wine, wandered out to the sun deck and gazed up at the stars. It seemed that there weren't as many as there were when he lived in Gastown. He wondered why. But so much had changed since the last century. Not being familiar with the science of astronomy, he thought that maybe this was some sort of process of evolution.

The moon was just a sliver in the sky. Another two or three weeks and it would once again be casting its glorious light as it had done the night he proposed to Margaret.

Margaret. Would he ever see her again? He remembered every detail of so well. Her smile, her beauty, the delicate scent of jasmine she wore.

Jonathan looked back into the living room. Kate had hung up the phone and was staring into space, rapidly tapping the pen she had been using on the pad. She did not look happy.

He walked into the room, sat on the back of the sofa and rubbed Kate's shoulders gently, feeling a shiver course through her under his touch. Quietly he asked, "Bad news?"

At first she didn't say anything, but the tapping stopped. Kate picked up her wineglass, took a sip, and let out a long sigh.

"That was my ex-husband. Allen."

Jonathan didn't know whether to pry further, but she was obviously disturbed. "Just calling to chat, was he?"

"I don't know what he wanted. It's the first time he's called me in almost a year."

"Perhaps he just wanted to see how you were," Jonathan offered, continuing his soothing massage.

Kate sighed again. "No. He wants something. He didn't have the guts to come right out and ask me, but he wants something. I can feel it."

Jonathan sensed her anger. It was through this man's actions that she now found herself in a difficult financial position, and it seemed that Allen should take responsibility in helping Kate out of her predicament.

"Has he offered to give you some assistance with the bank loan?" Jonathan asked.

"Ha!" Kate blurted out. "That would be the day. Besides, he's out of work again. It seems that he was fired from yet another law firm. Probably for embezzlement. He's such a crud!"

Crud? Jonathan wasn't familiar with the word, but he assumed that it was not a compliment. Kate was very upset. He had to do something to get her mind off the call.

He patted her on the shoulder. "I know what will make you feel better." Standing up, he said, "Come on. I discovered a marvelous little establishment down the block. We'll have a lovely glass of sherry, and the walk will do us both good."

Kate looked up at him and smiled briefly. She appreciated what he was trying to do, but she was not in the mood to go to a noisy pub.

"Thanks, but I think I'll just turn in. I wouldn't be very good company right now."

She got up slowly and walked down the hall to her bedroom. Turning back to him, she said, "I'm glad you had a good time tonight, Jonathan. I'll see you in the morning."

Kate closed her bedroom door and leaned against it, her mind spinning with the collection of events that had unfolded over the last week. As if her nerves weren't on edge enough with having Jonathan go to the gallery opening, the call from Allen had been the last straw.

As she began to undress, Kate decided that a long, hot bath might make her feel better. She poured her favourite jasmine scented bath foam under the steaming column of water.

She pulled a thick, rose coloured bath towel from the linen cupboard, turned toward the steaming tub and suddenly stopped. Jasmine. That was the scent she had smelled so strongly at the gallery tonight. Too tired to figure out the connection, if any, she finished getting ready for her bath.

Kate lit scented candles on the tile shelf that surrounded the Jacuzzi, and eased herself through the thick layer of crackling, white bubbles. She leaned against the sloping back of her soaker tub and sighed deeply.

Every muscle ached with tension. She felt drained, and stared blankly at the dancing flames of the candles.

What next?

Could her life get any more complicated?

She tried to let her mind go. To meditate on better times. But she was too wound up. After fifteen minutes, she decided that the only thing the hot bath was doing for her was turning her into a prune.

As she slipped into her favourite turquoise silk nightgown, Kate thought about the strange incidences at the party this evening. She had definitely felt someone push her. She shivered at the thought. It was getting harder and harder for her to not believe in ghosts.

Kate had never experienced anything like that in her life. Well, except for hearing Margaret's voice in the attic when she was young. But her mother had told her she was just hearing things.

But Kate had known at the time the voice was real, and she was just as sure now that someone, or something, had pushed her. Everything was connected somehow to Jonathan's arrival.

But how? Was it Margaret? And what was she trying to tell them?

Kate turned out the lamp on her bedside table, and stared at the waving shadows on the ceiling from the trees outside her window. Random thoughts wandered through her mind as she drifted to sleep.

KATE WALKED slowly into the sitting room. As she looked around, she realized that it was the main room of her gallery, but it wasn't her gallery. It was someone's home. She turned and saw a now familiar man across the room.

She felt Jonathan's eyes on her every step of the way. He was standing by the fire, his arm resting on the mantel of the fireplace.

Jonathan Wilks was one of the most attractive men she had ever met. His attire was impeccable, from his crisp, white linen shirt, finished with simple gold cuff links to the expensive wool pants that accentuated his fine build.

He had a sensuous aura that almost made it hard for Kate to breathe as she neared him. He extended his hand. As she took it, he drew her to him, then held her tight against his body.

"Margaret, I love you so much. So very much," Jonathan whispered against her ear.

Kate wanted to push away from him. To tell him that she was not Margaret, she was Kate. But she felt powerless in his warm embrace. She felt as if she had come home. Home from a very long journey, and that she was safe now. Safe with Jonathan.

She looked up at him. The firelight emphasized the strong, angular features of his handsome face. His blue eyes shone with love and desire. Kate wanted him. All of him. She wanted to be loved by him. To make love to him.

He gave her a knowing smile as he guided her to the antique settee in front of the fireplace, his arm still around her waist. They sat down, and Jonathan reached over to the carved oak coffee table, and poured a golden liquid into two crystal sherry glasses. Taking one himself and giving the other to her, he made a toast.

"To a love that shall live forever. Never will we be apart again, my love."

Kate lifted her delicate glass and touched the raised one in Jonathan's hand. The ping of fine crystal rang softly in the quiet room.

Neither spoke as they sipped their sherry. Jonathan gently held her hand, his eyes never leaving hers as he slowly stroked her palm with his thumb. The gesture sent rivers of sensual awakening coursing through her body. It had been a long time since she had made love to a man.

Jonathan took the small glass from Kate's hand and set it on the coffee table. He took her face in both his hands, and Kate could see his eyes focus on her mouth. Her lips parted in anticipation. Jonathan looked up at her again, as if silently asking permission. He must have read acceptance in her eyes.

Slowly, ever so slowly, he brought his lips to hers. The first touch was gentle. He drew back for a brief moment, then deepened the kiss as his hands left her face, and his arms wrapped tightly around her.

Kate slid her arms around Jonathan's neck, letting the sweet sensations, now totally out of her control, build inside her. She felt very lightheaded.

Jonathan trailed kisses across her cheek. Kate leaned back against the settee, lifting her face as Jonathan's lips explored the length of her neck.

"You are so beautiful," Jonathan said huskily as he once again gazed into Kate's eyes.

Kate felt like she was floating. Jonathan kissed her deeply, then swept her up in his arms. Kate wrapped her arms around his neck, leaning her face against the warm expanse of his shoulder. He smelled of sweet pipe smoke and spicy cologne.

He held her tightly as he carried her upstairs. Walking down the dimly lit hallway, he pushed open a door with his back and swung her into a room.

A tiffany oil lamp on the bedside table cast a soft glow in the room, creating a sheen on satin panels of the quilt. The iron frame of the small bed squeaked slightly as Jonathan gently laid Kate on to the thick covers.

He sat on the edge of the bed, his desire for her obvious in the look he gave her. Kate slowly ran her hand up his arm, extended across her to brace himself, and gently pulled him towards her.

For a moment, he resisted. Kate was confused.

Jonathan smiled lovingly at her. He brushed her cheek with the back of his hand. She felt his gaze go straight through to her soul.

"I do love you," he said, as if to reassure her that he was not taking the situation that was unfolding lightly.

Kate smiled back at him. "I know you do."

She had never felt so connected to anyone. She wanted to be with him for the rest of her life. The depth of her love for Jonathan seemed endless.

"There's something different about you tonight," Jonathan said. It was not a question, but a quiet statement. "You seem to be more alive than ever. I want to make love to you, Margaret. Please."

Kate felt as if she were drugged. Part of her wanted Jonathan to be saying her name, not Margaret's, but she gave in to the overwhelming desire, and moved over slightly to make room for him to lie beside her. She struggled to pull back the yards of fabric in her long dress.

Lying on his side, propped up on one arm, Jonathan's eyes never left

Kate's as he placed his hand on the gathered folds of material at her waist, then slowly moved his hand up to her breast. Kate gasped slightly as his thumb circled her already tightening nipple.

Jonathan leaned forward and kissed her again. Kate's own desire rose uncontrollably. She pulled him closer. Needing him. Wanting him. Again she felt as if she had been away from him for a very long time. Making love to Jonathan felt right.

Kate felt him undo the first of the row of pearlized buttons that ran down the bodice of her dress. With each button was an accompanying delicate kiss, first on her neck, and then slowly moving down as her bodice opened.

Jonathan raised his head, and unabashedly stared at the rise of Kate's breasts from the lacy corset she wore. "Beautiful," was all he said.

He traced one finger across the swell of each breast, then leaned down and kissed her lips as his finger continued the exquisite exploration.

Kate could hardly breathe. She wanted to make love to him. Immediately. With complete abandon.

But she felt dazed. Why was everything so fuzzy? She felt as if she was being pulled away from him. She tried to hold him closer, to take away the strange feeling. As if it was all an illusion, the room was starting to fade. Kate felt heavy. She could hear music.

Chapter 8

"...AND THE ninth caller will have an opportunity to win a trip for two to sunny Puerto Vallarta, compliments of CKOZ, Vancouver's favourite new music station. Come on all you sleepy heads! It's another bright and sunny day here on the West Coast. At eight-fifteen it's already creeping up to twenty degrees on the old Celsius meter."

Kate rolled over and slapped at the top of the clock radio until she found the snooze button. The annoying rapid-fire voice of the morning host was silenced. She wanted to get back to the dream. To continue making love to Jonathan.

But it was gone. Her mind was blank.

Yet her body still tingled from his imaginary touch. She had almost expected to find him beside her when she opened her eyes. But the other half of her bed was empty. Kate felt an odd sense of loss.

She shook off the strange feelings. This was ridiculous. She had been alone for way too long, but Jonathan Wilks was not the one to remedy that. He didn't even belong in this time. Did he?

After only one week, Kate couldn't imagine what her life had been like without Jonathan around.

Calmer. That's what it was. Jonathan had turned her world upside down. But he had also brought her back to life. She had been drowning in her own troubles with the bank. At least Jonathan had helped get her mind off that, for short periods of time.

But the fact remained that time was running out. She had to find a way to come up with more money. It would be so easy to let Jonathan sell his painting to Mrs. Sumner, but Kate was afraid that that would open a Pandora's box, creating more trouble than they could handle.

True, he had conducted himself well so far, but they still didn't know why he was here. Kate felt that until they did, it would be unwise to tempt fate.

The radio snapped on again, the melodic sounds of Anita Baker floating through the speaker. Kate threw back her covers and got out of bed. It was her turn to do the Saturday shift. She was due at the gallery at ten.

She could smell coffee. Jonathan must be up already. Kate felt a sense of awkwardness envelope her. Why had she been dreaming about him again? Dreaming in such vivid images of making love to him.

Kate slipped on her robe and wandered into the kitchen. Except for an empty coffee cup in the sink, Jonathan was nowhere in sight.

She found a note on the counter. "Gone for a walk."

Just as well, she thought, and went back to her room to get ready for work.

JONATHAN STROLLED along the sandy beach, his shoes in his hand. He had a lot of thinking to do, and being by the ocean seemed to help the process. He was falling in love with Kate Carston. Margaret's great, great, great granddaughter. Simply an impossible situation.

The dream he had had last night had seemed so real. It was as if he had been transported back to his own time. To Margaret. But it was Kate that he had been with. Had made love to. He hadn't had the courage to face her this morning. Surely he might have given his feelings away.

What he had really wanted to do was to hold her as she awakened. To feel her soft skin against his as the morning sun filtered through the window. To make love to her as he had done in the dream. To hear her call his name in the throes of passion.

The soft thumping of a morning jogger coming up behind him on the sand brought him out of his daydream. Jonathan was keenly aware of the contrast of sounds around him now. The rhythmic lapping of the waves on the shore, against the hum of the waking city.

Automobiles. A wonderful invention, yet seemingly the cause of great anxiety for those who used them.

People everywhere, but the friendly atmosphere that had abounded in the early days of Gastown no longer existed. People ignored each other on the streets. Never a courteous tip of the hat, not that many people even wore hats in this time. Except for the young ones. Odd to have the brim of one's hat used for shading the back of the neck.

Even those who did not use automobiles were always in such a hurry. Delivery boys on bicycles, going so fast through the city streets. It was a wonder they didn't do irreparable harm to the crowds they passed.

Jonathan wasn't sure that he liked being a part of it all, yet he had no choice but to try to fit in as best he could. He had thought a lot about Spencer Thomas's offer to write a newspaper column. He wanted to do it, if for no other reason than to help pay his own way. It simply would not do to have Kate support him in any way. Any man worth his salt would never let a woman take care of him financially.

Especially the woman he loved.

Jonathan stopped and faced the wind as it blew in along the shore.

He felt energized. He was going to get on with his new life. Starting with a job.

No matter what it took, he would get a permit to work, and he would begin his new life as a contributing member of this modern society.

Buoyed by his decision, he headed back to the condo, ready to take action.

FOUR HOURS later, Jonathan sat across the table from Spencer Thomas at a small cappuccino bar in the heart of Kitsilano's restaurant row. He was getting quite accustomed to the taste of the featured mocha lattes served at most of the busy cafes.

"Don't worry about what Kate thinks," Spencer said. "I think your outlook on art would be a refreshing addition to the paper."

Jonathan smiled. It was nice to finally be appreciated for his opinion on art. But there was the small matter of his work permit. Jonathan had decided to ask Spencer if he had any contacts to get the documents he needed.

"I am flattered by your offer, Spencer, however, it seems that there would be a small problem in that I do not have the required documents to work in your fine country."

"Are you just here on a visitor's visa?"

Jonathan hesitated. He had rehearsed his story repeatedly before deciding to give Spencer a call, but now that the moment of truth had arrived, he wasn't sure if he could go through with it in a believable fashion.

"Actually, I'm at a bit of a loss, as I do not have any papers at all," he replied, not quite able to look Spencer in the eye as he started his story. This was going to be harder than he had imagined.

Spencer eyed Jonathan over the top of his oversized coffee cup. He slowly placed the cup back on its saucer and sat back in his chair.

"Does Kate know about this?"

"Well, yes, but she made me promise not to tell anyone, lest it cause problems," Jonathan said.

Spencer chuckled lightly. "Yes, that it would." He leaned his arms on the table and looked directly at Jonathan. "Okay, let's have it then. What's your story?"

Jonathan took a deep breath and began the practiced lie. "Let's just say that it would not be a good idea if people knew what my real identity was. It's a little hard to explain."

Spencer was frowning. Jonathan began to feel his opportunity to make a contribution to his own life, as well as Kate's, might be slipping.

Quickly he continued.

"It's not as if I'm some sort of criminal. Quite the opposite. It's just that I'm not really supposed to be here."

Spencer's frown deepened. "Not supposed to be here? As in Vancouver here, or Canada?

Jonathan looked away. "Well...both. But I am, and I am truly interested in working with you on the newspaper, so all I have to do is get some identification. I know this is a large imposition to ask of you, but being as you are seemingly so well connected in this wonderful city, I thought perhaps you might..."

"Might know someone who can get you some fake ID?" Spencer finished the sentence. He sat back in his chair and blew out an extended breath. For a long moment he just stared at Jonathan, not saying a word.

Jonathan felt uncomfortable. It had seemed so easy for the man back in England to obtain the needed documents. Perhaps he was wrong in expecting this to be a simple procedure now. Spencer sat forward, his arms crossed in a defiant stance. Jonathan felt defeated. Had he just gotten himself, and Kate into more trouble?

"Kate is an important friend to me. If you have any intention of hurting her in any way, you are going to find yourself up against not only me, but many other people who care very much about her."

Jonathan had not expected that. Stunned, he sat forward in his chair and matched Spencer's cross-armed posture.

"I appreciate your concern, Spencer, but Kate means more to me than you know. I would never, not for one moment, let anything happen to her. As a matter of fact, she insisted that I forget about the idea of working for you. But the fact is, she is in need of financial help. And I am going to do everything I can to assist her. Even if I have to do so by means that need a little," he hesitated, "adjusting of my present circumstances."

Spencer's expression relaxed slightly as he sat back in his chair. "What do you mean, she needs financial help? I though the gallery was doing well."

Jonathan silently chastised himself for giving away such personal information about Kate, but now that it was out, perhaps Spencer would see the urgency in getting things settled so Jonathan could work.

"Please don't let on to her that I've told you anything, but it seems that her ex-husband left her high and dry, and although the gallery is doing well, Kate is struggling to make ends meet overall. I have to do something to help."

"Marrying Allen was a bad move from the start. I'm not surprised that he's caused Kate trouble." Spencer took another sip of his coffee.

Shaking his head as he placed his cup down, he chuckled. "I ought to have my head examined for even considering getting into this, but okay. Let me see what I can do. I used to have a contact, but I'm not sure if he's still around."

Jonathan felt as if he could burst. His plan was going to work. He knew it.

Spencer leaned forward, and in a low voice said, "Just tell me that you aren't in any trouble with the law, either here or in England."

He didn't have to lie. Raising his right hand, Jonathan replied, "I give you my word as an Englishman."

Spencer laughed. "Well, I'm not so sure your nationality has any bearing on it, but I will take your word."

More seriously, he added, "This is just between you and me, understand? If Kate, or anyone else asks, just say that you've made arrangements. That's all. Nothing else. We never had this conversation. Got it?"

"Got it. And thank you."

"No problem, but don't thank me until this is finished. As I said, I'm not even sure if this guy is still in town. In the mean time, maybe you can do your first assignment on spec."

Jonathan's elation faded slightly. "On spec? What type of show is that?"

Spencer rolled his eyes. "Spec. Speculation. A trial run. Just to see what you can produce. Maybe this arrangement won't work after all if you can't put what you see on paper."

For once in his life, Jonathan was glad that he paid some attention to the boring teachers in his endless studies. Of course he could put what he saw on paper. He was educated in one of the finest schools in England.

But Spencer need not know that. Jonathan would prove himself first hand.

"I'm sure you'll be pleasantly surprised with the results. Now. With which event would you like me to begin? On spec."

THE WEATHER had turned, and by Thursday, Kate was getting tired of summer rains, typical though for Vancouver. Today she busied herself with the final touches on restoring a painting found in an estate sale.

It was an early Ronini, a renowned local artist who passed away several years ago. Apparently the late owner had bought it from the painter in the 1940's, just after the war. Her husband had hated it, and it had remained in their attic until last month, when a lawyer had gone through the widow's effects. A forgotten treasure like that could have made a difference in the old woman's financial status.

Something like Jonathan's works. They had made a difference in Kate's life financially, when she had reluctantly sold off the first two of the treasured heirlooms.

But now she had the real thing. Jonathan Wilks. And his presence was doing anything but helping her financial status. Not to mention her mental stability. He had virtually stepped out of the favourite old photograph and changed her world. Since Jonathan's arrival, Kate decided to store that picture away, before anyone other than Jenny put two and two together.

Kate smiled as she thought back to years gone by when he had been a very big part of her life, although imaginary friends didn't count to the adult world.

He had been Kate's secret prince during her childhood years when she had played in the attic. The photograph of Jonathan and Margaret had always hung with reverence in what was then the main office of her grandmother's store.

Back then she had pretended that Jonathan would come over for tea. He would bow to her and to Mrs. Cranberry, her doll. The three of them, Kate, her best friend and doll, and her imaginary friend, Jonathan, would spent hours in the cozy attic, discussing world events. They debated how many more sleeps until Christmas, the loss of her teeth, and which of the splendid outfits in her grandmother's trunks would be best for the upcoming pretend ball, to which Jonathan would be her handsome escort and dancing partner. Kate once again recalled the soft scent of jasmine that had surrounded her tea parties.

Now he was here. In the flesh. And Kate wanted to do a lot more than dance with him. Her stomach tightened as she thought about the first time his arms circled her that day in her office. She closed her eyes and shook her head, willing away the thoughts. The last thing she needed right now was to get involved with a man who could vanish just as easily as he had appeared.

She had once been swept into a world of what turned out to be pretend love. Allen had not been the man she had believed him to be. Nothing good had come of the marriage, except giving her the push to renovate the gallery, thinking it would be part of their future together.

Now her future was completely up in the air. She had sold a few more pieces, enough to cover the bank expenses for this month, but she couldn't keep up this battle with time forever. She needed a miracle.

With a short tap on the door, Jenny joined Kate in the private work area. She had a pot of tea in one hand and a sandwich in the other.

"Hi. You've been up here for hours. I thought you might like a break."

Kate put down her paintbrush, and stretched. She hadn't realized she had been at it for so long. Now that she stopped, her back ached from bending over the antique piece of art.

"Thanks for looking after me, Jen. You're a pal," Kate said, genuinely appreciative of her assistant's effort.

"So how's it going?" Jenny asked, leaning against the doorframe as she sipped her own tea.

"Fine. How's it going with you?" Kate returned, knowing that Jenny's question was more than just casual banter.

"Don't give me that. You know what I'm talking about. You're in love, Kate Carston."

Kate feigned surprise as she swallowed a bite of her sandwich. She pretended her mouth was still full, and just pointed at herself.

Jenny laughed. "Yes, you. There's enough electricity going on between you and Jonathan to light up the entire street for a month!"

Kate could feel the tint of blush rise in her cheeks. Was it that obvious?

"It's a totally impossible situation, Jen. I mean, the man is over a hundred and sixty years old!"

"So? Older men are more experienced," Jenny replied, laughing.

"Besides. He could vanish into thin air at any moment. We still have no idea how he got here, or why. He's driving me crazy, too."

"Why?"

Kate groaned as she stood up and walked to the window. She leaned against the sill and took another sip of tea.

"Everything is getting out of control. The harder I try to keep him under wraps, the more people want a part of him. Mrs. Sumner. Spencer. Even Lisa. Have you noticed she's been *dropping by* the gallery a lot more often in the past couple of weeks?"

The tinkling sounds of the chimes that hung over the front door of the gallery ended their conversation.

Jenny stood to go downstairs, then turned back to Kate. "Don't worry. Everything will work out. He's doing fine so far. He seems to care about you a lot. I'm sure he won't purposely do anything to upset you," she said as she headed out the door to look after the arriving customer.

Kate watched Jenny leave. "Not purposely," she said to the empty room.

Just as Kate was about to get back into the restoration job, Jenny called to her from the bottom of the staircase.

"Kate? Could you come here for a minute?"

Kate didn't want any more interruptions. She needed to get this job finished. She walked over to the railing and looked down to the main gallery lounge.

A woman stood by the window, looking up at her. Kate had seen the woman before, but wasn't sure where. Jenny's face was etched with concern.

"Kate, this is Clarice. She's the lady who does tarot card readings across the street at the cafe," Jenny said, obviously as confused as Kate by the woman's presence.

As Kate went down the stairs, Clarice stared intently. Something was wrong. Kate could almost feel the tension emanating from the woman.

"Is there something I can do for you?" Kate asked, trying to remain nonchalant. But inside, every nerve was on edge. This was just another example of strange occurrences that had become commonplace since Jonathan's arrival.

"I must talk with you," Clarice said, her voice low.

Jenny had been to Clarice several times over the years for readings, and Kate looked to her for a clue as to what was going on. Jenny merely shrugged, her face still showing a mixture of confusion and concern.

Kate motioned toward the sofa. "Please, have a seat."

As Kate joined her, Clarice looked around the gallery's lower floor, then stared up at the balcony area.

Jenny started to walk to the back office. "If you need anything, I'll be back here," she said quietly to Kate as she left the room.

Kate nodded, turning back to Clarice.

Laughing nervously, Kate said, "I've never had a house call from a psychic before. Can I get you a coffee or anything?"

Clarice smiled briefly, but her face still showed deep concern. "Thank you, no. I must tell you that I am not in the habit of doing, as you say, *house calls* either, but for the last few days, I have had visions of this gallery, of you, and of a man I have never seen before. I cannot seem to stop them."

Now Kate was beginning to worry. Was she picking up on Jonathan?

"What kind of visions?" Kate questioned.

"That's the problem. I can usually see things for people so clearly. But that is when people come to me to have a reading. In this case, I am only seeing fragments of people, of events. You have never been to see me, yet these images are constant. I felt compelled to come to you. This has never happened," Clarice replied, twisting the large aquamarine ring on her right hand as she spoke.

"Look, I've never really been much of a believer in psychic stuff," Kate began, although the last two weeks definitely given her cause to re-examine her opinions.

Before she could continue, Clarice looked directly into her eyes, seemingly seeing right through her.

"There is a presence here. Something has changed in the last while. There is a woman. I would almost say it is you, but she is in spirit form. And a man."

Kate froze. She could be in trouble if Clarice really could sense something going on, she could be trouble. Thank goodness Jonathan had decided to play tourist for the day and wasn't hanging around the gallery. Come to think of it, Jonathan had not spent much time at the gallery at all this week.

"Okay, not that I'm saying I believe in all of this," Kate said, trying to sound casual, "but what exactly are you seeing?"

Clarice closed her eyes, as if trying to see the images she was referring to. After several moments, she opened her eyes and looked directly at Kate.

"You are having some financial difficulties."

Kate's mouth dropped open. How could she have possibly known that?

"There is a dark haired man who is involved somehow."

A dark haired man? The bank manager had dark hair. But so did Jonathan. So did Allen. So did any number of men that Kate knew.

"Your husband, the artist, where is he?" Clarice asked.

Kate was confused. "I'm divorced, and my ex-husband was not an artist. You must be mistaken."

"No, there is a man. An artist. He loves you very much. I can feel a love so great it transcends all boundaries. Are you seeing someone?"

Kate couldn't tell her about Jonathan. Maybe Clarice could give them some insight as to why Jonathan was here, as Jenny had suggested on the first day he arrived, but Kate wasn't ready for that yet.

Avoiding her question, Kate asked, "Where is all of this coming from? I mean, this is very unusual. Do all psychics just get these images popping into their brain out of the blue?"

"As I said," Clarice replied quietly, "this has never happened to me before. But it is something I cannot ignore. Particularly since I feel that there is a danger of some kind."

Kate's stomach clenched. She wasn't sure of what her future held, but danger?

"What do you mean?"

"I'm not sure. All I know is that there is a man with dark hair. He is tall. I wish I could be more sure of what I am seeing, but it is more of a feeling at the moment. A woman in a long dress is around you. Do you know who that might be?"

Margaret. Kate shuddered. It was all coming together. But she couldn't let Clarice know about Jonathan. Not yet.

"Look, Clarice, I'm not saying that I don't believe you, but I'm really not sure what you're referring to. Maybe it's just the full moon coming up, or something," Kate said smiling and standing up, hoping to dissuade Clarice from digging any further.

Clarice expression didn't change, but as she rose from the couch, she stared for a moment at the upper floor of the gallery again.

Suddenly the jasmine scent returned. Clarice looked directly at the empty space to the right of Kate, then looked straight into her eyes.

"She is with you, the woman in the dress. She will help you. But be careful. The road ahead will not be easy."

Chapter 9

JONATHAN WAS on his third cup of coffee. He was sure he'd been stood up. He looked at his pocket watch again, then watched the people outside scurry by, umbrellas up. Although still warm, it had been raining for three days now.

Three-fifteen.

Ten minutes from the last time he'd looked. Jonathan didn't like the feel of this at all. He would give the man another fifteen minutes.

All week long he had been trying to keep himself busy, out of Kate's way. He was so excited about the possibility of getting his new identification that he was sure he might blurt out something to give away his plans.

He knew Kate would thoroughly disapprove of what he was doing, and would try to prevent it. But nothing could stop him now. Spencer had been quite impressed with the article Jonathan had written on the *Celebration of Human Revolution* show that had taken place last Sunday. Human revulsion was more like it, Jonathan thought. A disgusting display of nudity in the name of art.

Although, as a fellow artist, Jonathan had to respect their sense of direction, and had given them a decent enough offering in his piece. He liked writing. It was something that he had never been given an opportunity to do, but now that he had, he felt he could confidently work for the Kitsilano Courier and Spencer Thomas.

If he could ever get some proper identification, that is. And if this meeting did not take place, those papers might never be realized. This must work. Kate needed him.

Just as he was about to give up, an ordinary looking man walked through the front door and headed straight toward the booth Jonathan occupied.

They had picked a small, old cafe on the outskirts of Gastown to meet. One that was not old enough to be too seedy, but not new enough to be busy with tourists or business people.

Two days previously, Jonathan had given the man one thousand dollars of the precious advance Spencer had offered. Spencer knew that the identification would cost Jonathan twenty-five hundred dollars, and had loaned him the money against future wages for his writing. Jonathan was afraid the man would take his money and disappear, but Spencer had assured him he would come through.

The man never did give his name, something Jonathan was not comfortable with at all, but he was finally here.

The man sat down without a word, signaling to the waitress that he did not want to order anything. "Hey," he said to Jonathan as he settled into the corner of the booth bench seat.

Jonathan was getting used to modern slang terms, and returned the curt greeting.

"Hey. I trust that you have come to conclude our business proposition," he asked, trying not to sound over anxious.

The man reached inside his jacket and pulled out a small manila envelope. Placing it on the table, he slid it across to Jonathan.

Jonathan felt as if there were dozens of eyes on them, on the transaction that was being made, but as he looked around the small cafe, he noted that the only other person in the room was a very disinterested waitress who was engrossed in a paperback novel.

Nervously, he opened the envelope and peered inside. There, at the bottom were two small items—his birth certificate and social insurance card. It didn't seem like a lot for the amount of money he was paying, yet it was everything in the world to Jonathan. He was a real person. Jonathan Edward Westham.

It saddened him to think that he could never again be Jonathan Wilks, but it was a small price to pay for the privilege, indeed the necessity of being able to work, to take care of Kate, and to show her that he was a man worth his stock. That he was a man she could count on.

Jonathan beamed at the nameless man across the booth from him. "Thank you. You have no idea how much this means to me."

"Yeah, yeah. Where's my money," the man replied gruffly, totally unmoved by Jonathan's enthusiasm.

Jonathan reached into his jacket pocket, and pulled out a wad of bills. After ensuring the waitress was still buried in her novel, he handed the money across the table.

The man flipped through the bills quickly, satisfied that the proper amount was there.

"It's been a slice," he said, preparing to leave the booth.

Jonathan reached out and put his hand on the man's arm. For his efforts, he was met with a cold, warning look. He quickly withdrew his hand.

"I just want to say thanks again. If I am ever in need of—"

"Look, buddy. This is it. I don't know you, I ain't never seen you, and I ain't never had any business with you. Got it? And you ain't never heard of me. Got it?" the man growled, keeping his voice low.

Jonathan realized that this was not the time to extend the etiquette standard in most personal and business transactions he had ever been involved with.

"Got it," he replied, casually leaning back into the corner of the booth as the other man had done.

Jonathan watched as the man lumbered across the room and out the door into the rainy street, then looked once more inside the envelope.

He smiled triumphantly. He was a real person.

KATE HATED the fact that she was beginning to look for little signs in Jonathan that would in any way connect him with the warning from Clarice.

For almost a week, though, he had been out late, saying he had just been down at the local tavern playing darts with a few blokes he'd taken up with. He had barely spent any time working on his paintings, which up until now had seemed to give him such a sense of contentment.

Something was wrong.

He hadn't even mentioned the offer from Spencer again. Not that that was bad. It saved Kate the agony of having to worry that he would be mixing with the one person who might see through his story.

But she missed him.

She missed seeing his determination to fit in to modern day life. She missed the way the dimple in his left cheek was deeper than in his right cheek. The way his eyes would light up when he learned something new, or felt an accomplishment in mastering simple things like revolving doors. She missed his strong hugs, ensuring her that she had nothing to worry about, that he was fitting in nicely.

But the nagging voice of worry would not go away. What if some of his little trips were setting him up for danger to himself?

She wouldn't mention Clarice's warning. Not yet. Maybe she was wrong. Until a couple of weeks ago, Kate didn't believe in psychics at all. Why now was she putting so much into one simple statement from a woman she had never met before?

Maybe tonight she would just sit Jonathan down and find out what was going on, whether she had anything to be genuinely concerned about. It was probably nothing. He was probably just out having fun.

The front door chimes tinkled, bringing Kate out of her dark thoughts. Jenny had asked for the afternoon off, so Kate was busier than usual. She smiled at the customer, pushing her worries about Jonathan to the back of her mind. For now.

JONATHAN HAD been pacing the entire floor of the condo for almost an hour. Jenny would be here any minute. In only a few short hours, Jonathan would be sitting with Kate enjoying a romantic candlelight dinner, and would be able to give her the good news. She would be so pleased.

The doorbell rang. "Finally", he said.

"Thank goodness! I was beginning to think you might not arrive safely," he blurted as he swung the door open wide.

Jenny walked into the foyer, laughing as she fumbled with four bags of groceries. She had been only too pleased to secretly help Jonathan prepare an elegant dinner for two to help them celebrate. She wasn't sure what it was that they were celebrating, but Jonathan had been so eager to create a night that Kate would never forget, Jenny couldn't resist.

They had gone over menu ideas, settling on a simple beef casserole with vegetables. Something that Jonathan could handle on his own, once Jenny helped him get everything in the oven and had given lengthy instructions on using the microwave to do the final cooking. She had gone to Chez Bonbon to pick up Kate's favourite pavlova for dessert.

By five o'clock, everything was basically done. All Jonathan had to do once Kate arrived was put the vegetables in the microwave, light the candles, serve the imported French red wine, already uncorked to breathe, and serve dinner.

Simple.

Kate was bound to be impressed. And Jenny was dying to find out what the big news was, but Jonathan had been very tight lipped. He gave her a hug as he escorted her to the door, telling her that she would find out soon enough.

WHEN KATE walked in, her senses were surrounded with delicious smells and soft music—an atmosphere that had been absent in her home for a very long time.

Jonathan gathered her into his arms without a word, and before she could say anything, lowered his head and kissed her gently. Kate swayed in his arms to the rhythm of the gentle sounds coming from the stereo. She was swept away, totally and completely. As she looked up, Jonathan's gaze went straight to the depths of her soul.

He smiled and quietly said, "Welcome home."

Kate felt as if she had been waiting for this moment all her life. As if she had finally come home. And he was here. Her childhood prince. The man she dreamed of finding all her teen years, just like Margaret had. She wanted to be with Jonathan, to share her life with him. To love him and make love to him. Just like in the dreams.

She smiled and touched his face. "This is a surprise." Inhaling deeply, she said, "It smells like you've been busy."

Jonathan locked his fingers behind her waist and grinned. "Well, I must admit that I had a little help."

"Jenny?"

"Yes. I hope things weren't too busy at the gallery this afternoon for you."

Kate shook her head, laughing. "The little sneak. She told me she had to take care of some family business."

"I think she considers you family. In any case, she was most helpful. I am now a qualified casserole chef, and Jenny assured me that I wouldn't have too much trouble finishing things off myself."

Kate stepped away from his embrace and further into the room, taking the ambiance that had been so carefully created. Table elegantly set for two, using her best china, fresh bread, colourful salad in a large glass bowl, tongs crossed neatly atop, linen napkins with brass rings sitting on each plate, and a beautiful bouquet of flowers. It was perfect.

She turned back to him, and he took both of her hands. He hoped the rest of the night would continue like this. He felt deliriously happy. He wanted to go out on the sun deck and shout with joy to anyone who would listen. *I, Jonathan Wilks, have found the most wonderful woman on the face of this great earth! I love Kate Carston! Do you hear me world?*

Instead he bent forward and kissed her lightly again, drawing her into his arms once more. As he held her, he felt it was time to give her the good news.

"I have a surprise for you," he whispered against her ear.

He drew back to gauge her reaction. She looked suitably puzzled. He reached into his pants pocket and drew out the documents he had received. Stepping back from her, he held out the small cards and waited.

Kate took them, her frown increasing as she looked at each one. Jonathan's enthusiasm faltered slightly.

"Where on earth did these come from?" she questioned.

From the look on her face, Jonathan wasn't quite sure if she was angry, or just very confused. He hoped for the latter. Smiling brightly, he said, "I am official. I am a real person."

Kate was stunned. How did he get these? Who had he been dealing with that could get him such perfect looking identification. They read, 'Jonathan Edward Westham', the name he had obviously settled on.

Jonathan answered her unspoken questions. "I can't tell you where I got them, but now I can work for Spencer without causing him any problems. I am legal."

"Does Spencer know about this?"

"Well, yes, actually. He—" Kate probably realized Spencer was the one who had set it up, but the less she knew about how this incident transpired, the better.

She didn't know what to say. This sort of thing was done all the time, but not with anyone she had ever known, much less someone she was in love with. What would the consequences be if anyone found out?

"Jonathan, this is…is…"

"Quite illegal. Yes, I know. But it is something that had to be carried out."

"But what if someone found out?" Kate searched Jonathan's face for an answer. Sighing, she said, "I suppose it really is the only answer, now that you've started this thing with Spencer. Besides, it's not like you're stealing or anything."

"Right," Jonathan agreed.

"I mean, it's not like you could go through any legal means, even if you wanted to."

"Right."

Kate laughed nervously. "Besides, if we told the truth, they'd lock both of us up. Right?"

"Right." Jonathan took the documents out of her hand and placed them on the counter. "Please Kate, this is a night of celebration. I have some things to tell you that, after you think about them, I'm sure you will be just as pleased as I am. I even have your favourite dessert," he said, opening the fridge door to reveal the scrumptious pavlova waiting to be served.

He moved to the table and poured two glasses of red wine. Passing one to Kate, he raised his in a toast. "To our future, whatever it may hold."

Kate raised her glass to meet his. *Ping.* She wanted their future to be together, whatever it held. He had been brought to her, by a power she dared not think about, but was eternally grateful to.

The evening went flawlessly. Kate reveled in having someone cook a meal in her own home, and she did not lift a finger to prepare, serve, or clean up after. Jonathan catered to her every need.

The subject of his identification had been put aside for the time being. Kate didn't want to ruin the magic by worrying about how he managed to come up with such important documents, although forged.

After dinner, they moved to the living room, and in front of the glowing fire, hardly needed because it was still summer, relaxed with a glass of well-aged port. Jonathan draped his arm across the back of the sofa and moved closer to Kate. She leaned her head against his shoulder, listening to the wonderful tone of his voice quietly telling her stories of days gone by.

Kate reached for her pendant, running her finger over the edges of the zigzag cut. It felt so natural sitting here with Jonathan. He began a slow massage of her neck, sending vibrations of wanting coursing through her. She turned to look up at him, and saw a burning desire in his eyes that mirrored her own.

Her lips parted in anticipation, as he lowered his head towards her. A deep fire inside Kate ignited as soon as the kiss began, unleashing the passion that had bubbled to the surface so many times before, only to be tamped out by circumstances. He tasted like red wine, cream and kiwi fruit from the pavlova. Kate's body tingled. She wanted to feel his arms holding her tight. To feel his hands exploring her body. As he had done in her dreams.

Jonathan deepened the kiss, his tongue probing into the sweetness that was Kate. He had never wanted a woman so badly in all his years. She pulled him closer, returning the kiss with an intensity that sent Jonathan over the edge.

Not breaking the kiss he lay back on the full-length sofa, pulling her with him so she was lying against him. She shuddered as he caressed her back, then ran his hand over the firm curve of her hip. Jonathan felt the heat rising between them. His hand moved slowly up her body, and as he neared her breasts, she turned slightly, letting him know that she wanted to be touched.

Pulling away from the kiss, Jonathan whispered, "You are incredible." The love that shone from Kate's eyes gave him all the encouragement he needed. Shifting their bodies so they were almost side by side, Jonathan lowered his head and kissed her deeply until they were both breathless. His hand once again slid slowly up her stomach, and she gasped as he cupped her breast.

"Oh, Jonathan, I want you," Kate cried out as she fumbled with the buttons on his shirt.

Jonathan answered with a crushing kiss, his breathing ragged as he felt the softness of Kate's delicate hand caress his exposed chest.

"Margaret. Oh, how I've waited for this moment," he said.

He realized his faux pas as Kate's body went very still. The magic was gone. In a single word, he had managed to undo everything he had planned so carefully tonight.

"Kate, I am so sorry."

Colors of Time

With a heavy sigh, she pushed away from him. Looking away, she said, "No big deal." Her tone of voice indicated otherwise, as did the fact that she got up from the couch, took her glass of sherry and walked out to the sun deck.

Jonathan raked his fingers through his hair and groaned. How could he have made such a mistake. Yes, he still loved Margaret, but that was over one hundred years ago. Now he was here with Kate...alive.

He picked up his sherry and followed her outside. Placing his glass on the patio table, he walked up behind Kate and slid his arms around her waist, pulling her closely against his chest. He was thankful she didn't resist.

They stood together for a long while, neither one speaking. The lights of Grouse Mountain shone in the dark sky beyond the city. Crickets buzzed from a nearby thicket that ran along the perimeter of the complex.

Jonathan placed his hands on Kate's shoulders and turned her to face him. He had to make her understand. With one finger, he raised her chin so she would have to look at him directly. "You, Kate Carston, have saved my life, in a way. I wanted this evening to be something special we could share, to mark the beginning of our future. Yes, I loved, or perhaps I should say love Margaret. As far as my mind is concerned, I saw her just a short time ago. But we both know that is not true."

Kate looked away but he turned her face toward him again.

"I want you to be with me for as long as I am here, in this time. I—"

The ringing phone stopped Jonathan. Kate started to go inside.

"Let your answering device pick up a message," he pleaded, pulling her close.

"Hello, Ms. Carston, this is Constable Venables of the Vancouver Police. Could you please call us immediately at the—"

Kate pushed away from Jonathan's embrace and ran inside. Grabbing the phone, she almost yelled, "Hello! This is Kate. What's wrong?" she asked fearfully.

The even toned voice of the policeman continued. "Good evening, Ms. Carston. We're going to need you to come down to your gallery as soon as possible."

"Why?"

"There's been a break-in. Several pieces of art have been stolen."

Chapter 10

BY THE TIME Kate and Jonathan arrived at the gallery, the police had already cordoned off the entrance with yellow tape. A small crowd of curious onlookers gathered outside, peering in at the activities of the policemen at work.

Kate parked her car behind one of the police cruisers and put on her emergency flashers.

"Excuse me, ma'am, you can't park there," a policeman said gruffly as he approached her..

"This is my gallery," Kate answered as she ignored his outstretched arm and headed toward the front door.

The policeman stepped out of her way. "Then you'll have to speak to Constable Venables. He's over there by the stairwell."

Jonathan nodded to the officer and put his hand on Kate's shoulder as they entered the gallery.

Kate approached the officer by the stairs. "Excuse me," she said, trying to keep the panic out of her voice. "What happened? When did someone get in here?"

The officer turned to Kate. "Are you the owner?"

"Yes. I'm Kate Carston. Please, what is going on here?"

Constable Venables looked around the gallery briefly before answering, flipping his notebook closed.

"Well, we got a call about an hour ago. One of the staff members from the restaurant across the street saw a couple of guys in here. They said the men had some of the lights on and were taking pictures from the wall. Since they didn't seem to be in any hurry, the witness didn't think much of it."

"What did these men look like?" Kate asked, totally confused.

"We don't know. There weren't many lights on, and since the witness didn't think anything was wrong at first, they didn't pay that much attention."

"What made them call you?" Jonathan asked, pulling Kate closer. He noticed she had begun to shake.

The officer shrugged. "I guess someone else at the restaurant knew the place was run by women and got suspicious. By the time they called us, it was too late. The mystery men had helped themselves."

Kate put a trembling hand to her mouth. "I don't believe this is happening."

"Well somebody knew what they were after, and it would seem that they knew the place well enough to get in and out without tripping the alarm. It was deactivated when we arrived. Who knows the code to your alarm system?" Constable Venables asked.

Kate's mind reeled. She had only given the security code out to her most trusted employees. Surely none of them would be involved in this?

Her legs began to wobble. Kate felt Jonathan's arm encircle her waist and she leaned into him, not sure if she would be able to stand much longer.

He led her over to the sofa and took her hand as they sat down. Kate felt her throat tighten as she tried to hold back the threatening tears.

Constable Venables joined them on the sofa. "I know this must be very upsetting for you, Ms. Carston, but we're going to need a statement. We will also need a list of the missing pieces. Will your insurance cover this?"

Kate looked around the gallery in a daze. There were blank spots everywhere. Her most expensive pieces were gone. Her heart leapt to her throat as she focused on a spot half way up the stairwell. Her hand flew to her chest as a tightness virtually took her breath away.

"What is it, my love?" Jonathan asked frantically, pulling her closer to him.

Kate could only point to the blank spot on the stairwell wall.

Jonathan's heart sank as he realized that the missing piece was one of his. The one Kate had been working on the day he had arrived at her back door. A myriad of emotions washed over him.

He turned to Kate and saw the tears threatening to spill over. He couldn't bear to see the pain in her eyes.

"Oh, Jonathan," she said, her voice trembling. "What am I going to do? Most of the missing pieces were either sold or had been spoken for. If the insurance doesn't cover them, I won't be able to pay the mortgage. I'll lose the gallery for sure!"

Kate gave in to the tears, burying her face against Jonathan's shoulder. This was the final blow. All of the pressures of trying to keep the wolves away from the door came crashing down around her.

Jonathan held her tightly as sobs racked her slim body. He felt helpless. He could do nothing at the moment. Except to hold her. To hope that his love for her would give them enough strength to carry on.

They would, and indeed, could overcome this terrible incident, he vowed.

"There, there, my love," Jonathan comforted, hugging her tightly again. "Don't fret. We'll get through this. I promise." He stroked her hair as the sobs settled slowly to sniffles. Her body still trembled. He wanted to just hold her like this for the rest of the night, to make everything better.

The emotionless voice of the police officer broke the moment. "Ms. Carston, this will only take a short time, then you can be on your way home."

For the next hour, Kate went through the gallery with Constable Venables, making a list of the missing pieces, including the computer from her office. She never kept any money on site as most of her sales were done by check or credit card.

Jonathan stayed by her side constantly. Kate was thankful for that. She needed him. He was a part of her life now. And a part of her heart.

After they had completed the inventory, Constable Venables turned to Jonathan. "Could I get your name, sir?" he asked, pen poised above his notebook.

Kate and Jonathan exchanged a fleeting glance.

Jonathan stood up tall and squared his shoulders. "My name is Jonathan Westham," he replied, proudly acknowledging his new official name.

As he wrote in his notebook, the officer asked, "Do you have any identification?"

Jonathan beamed inwardly. Trying not to sound overly smug, he said, "Yes, officer. I—" His heart skipped a beat as he reached into his empty pants pocket.

"Oh, damn!" he cursed, frantically searching all pockets in his pants and shirt.

Kate came to his rescue. "We left in such a hurry. His wallet must be still sitting at home on the coffee table."

Constable Venables stopped writing, looking from Kate to Jonathan. "Where do you live?" he asked, looking directly at Jonathan.

"Twelve sixty-five Maple Avenue, apartment three sixteen," Kate answered before Jonathan could get a word in.

Flipping his notebook back several pages, Constable Venables looked at Kate. "You two live together?"

"Yes," Kate answered tiredly, reaching for Jonathan's hand. Well, it wasn't a lie, she rationalized. They were living at the same address. She just wanted this night to end so they could go home.

Jonathan's hand tightened over Kate's. As she looked into his eyes, loving warmth spread through her as it had done so often over the past few days.

Constable Venables continued to write. Looking up briefly, he asked Jonathan, "So are you one of the people who has access to the security code?"

Again, Kate spoke up. "No, he doesn't. Besides, he was with me all night."

Without looking up from his notebook, Constable Venables asked, "And where were you before you got the call to come down here?"

He looked up when he didn't receive an immediate reply. Noticing the crimson flush on both Kate and Jonathan's faces, he said, "Oh. Never mind."

Kate and Jonathan both tried to speak at the same time.

"No! It's not what..." Kate stammered.

"I can assure you, officer, that—" Jonathan spoke quickly over Kate.

The officer held up his hand, silencing them both. "Hey, none of my business. Thank you for your time. We'll wait until you reset the alarm, Ms. Carston, then tomorrow you'll have to get in touch with your insurance agent. Here's my card, and the case file number. The insurance agency will need it to start your claim."

By the time Kate and Jonathan got home it was one o'clock in the morning. Kate dropped her keys on the coffee table and slumped on to the sofa, totally drained.

She stared unseeing across the room, her mind numb. She whispered, "What am I going to do?"

Jonathan sat beside her and gathered her into his arms. The minutes ticked by as they sat in silence.

He lifted her face to meet his. "We'll get through this. Together. I promise," he said then leaned down to kiss her lightly. Her head fell against his shoulder as she released a long, shuddering sigh.

Kate reached out to intertwine her fingers with his. "Please stay with me tonight, Jonathan," she whispered.

He hugged her tightly in response. "Anything you want, my love. I will always be here for you," he said, hoping with all of his heart that it would be true, that he would not disappear just as mysteriously as he had arrived.

Slowly he stood, gently pulling Kate up with him. Holding hands, they silently walked down the hall to her bedroom.

"I'm just going to wash up," Kate said.

Staring at her reflection in the wall-to-wall bathroom mirror, she could see the strain of the last few months had finally caught up with her. Dark circles hung below her eyes. She had lost weight, her face hollow at the cheeks. She sat on the edge of the tub and buried her face in her hands as tears flowed freely once more.

How much more could she take? Was it all really worth fighting so hard for?

"You must save our home," a woman's voice whispered.

Startled, Kate looked up quickly. The room was empty, but the jasmine scent had returned.

"Margaret?" Kate asked, but there was no reply.

She filled the sink with tepid water and began to wash her face. As she bent over to rinse off the cleanser, she heard the whisper again.

"Jonathan will help you," the woman said.

Kate whirled around, droplets of water still running down her face. Again, there was nobody there. But this time she was sure she had heard the voice.

"Margaret," Kate whispered. There was no reply.

She quickly changed and went back into the bedroom. Jonathan was sitting on the edge of her bed.

His gaze swept over her, pure desire shining in his eyes. Kate pulled her black silk dressing gown close around her as she slowly walked toward the bed.

Jonathan offered his hand and Kate went to him, feeling the warmth of his touch as he closed his hand around hers and gently pulled her down to sit beside him.

She wanted to tell him about hearing Margaret, but held back. Tonight Kate wanted Jonathan to be with her, and with her alone. She slid her fingers through the long, silky strands of his thick hair, and pulled him toward her. Her lips parted in anticipation, needing to taste him, to feel his arms around her, to feel his hands exploring every inch of her body.

He did not disappoint her.

From the first touch, the fire was ignited. Kate could not have stopped kissing him if she had wanted to. The connection went beyond the physical. It was as if she was being transported into an abyss of pure ecstasy.

Kate felt his hands roaming up and down the smooth fabric covering her back while his tongue danced hungrily with hers. Jonathan slowly removed her gown, sliding it off her shoulders to reveal the thin straps of the royal blue satin teddy she always wore to bed. His lips never left hers as he trailed his thumbs along each of her shoulders, making Kate shiver under his touch.

She heard his throaty moan as he slipped her dressing gown over her arms. His hands slid back up her body, stopping at her breasts, cupping, squeezing and circling each of the hardened peaks.

Jonathan stopped briefly, only long enough to lift Kate to the middle of the queen size bed, then continued exploring the curves of her neck with butterfly kisses.

"My Lord, Kate, you are driving me mad," Jonathan whispered huskily, slipping his thumb under one strap of her teddy and sliding it over her shoulder, following the route of his hands with more kisses.

Kate felt her entire body tingling, waiting eagerly for his hands to find each spot that craved the attention he was so willing to provide. She gasped as she felt his mouth close over her right nipple, suckling gently at first, then taking her greedily as his left hand roamed over her hips, and down her leg.

As his hand slowly traversed back up her leg, Kate arched her back, all of her senses screaming for Jonathan to take her, to fill her body with his. His hand brushed over the junction of her thighs, making Kate cry out.

"Oh, Jonathan, yes!"

"Tell me, my darling Kate. Tell me what you desire."

Kate felt as if she was floating, just as she had in the dreams where she came so close to making love to Jonathan. Now he was here, in her bed, and his touch was very real, and more exciting than anything Kate had ever experienced.

Instead of telling him, Kate boldly covered his left hand with hers and guided it under the lace edge of her teddy. Her entire body contracted as his fingers made contact with the moistness. Pushing aside the fabric, he continued manipulating her towards an explosion of passion unlike she had ever experienced.

Kate needed to feel him, all of him, and frantically pulled at the buttons on his shirt as he pulled her teddy down and over her hips, exposing her completely to him.

He shrugged out of his shirt, and as Kate's hands moved to undo his belt, he stopped her. Both were breathing heavily, both filled with uncontrollable urges that need to be satisfied, but Jonathan held firm to Kate's hands.

Confused, she looked into his eyes, finding nothing other than desire as great as her own shining back. "What's wrong?" she asked, barely above a whisper.

Jonathan stared at the full length of Kate's naked body. "Nothing. Absolutely nothing. I just wanted to savor this moment. You are so very beautiful, Kate, and if something were to happen that I might not stay here, in this time, I want to remember everything about you."

"Oh, Jonathan," Kate began, but her words were muffled as he claimed her mouth again, allowing her to continue undressing him. As she lowered the zipper, she could feel the extent of his readiness through the thin fabric of his briefs.

He sat up briefly and with swift movements, peeled the rest of his clothing off. Lying on his back, he pulled Kate up to straddle him, her hands gripping his shoulders for balance.

Their gazed locked as Jonathan stroked her slim, round bottom, sliding his hands along the outside of her upper legs and back to find the wetness he had previously discovered. Kate's body writhed above his. She reached down to stroke his manhood, now hard and pulsating with need.

"I need you, Kate. I need you right now," Jonathan demanded, reaching up with both hands and squeezing her breasts.

"Yes, Jonathan, yes. Please."

Jonathan rolled Kate on her back, and positioned himself between her thighs.

"Now, Jonathan. Please, I want you so bad."

Jonathan plunged his full length into her, feeling her legs wrap around his waist, claiming him. He heard her moan, then began to slowly slide out of her, only to feel her legs tighten around him, pulling him back inside.

Soon he could no longer hold back. Exploding inside her, Jonathan collapsed on top of Kate's already satiated body. He let out a long, contented sigh as Kate's delicate hands stroked his back.

Kate reveled in the sensations that enveped her. The weight of Jonathan's body on hers, the tender touch of his lips on her shoulders. He moved to lie on his side and pulled her into a warm, protective embrace without a word.

Nothing needed to be said. Kate could feel everything he wanted to say, and knew that he could sense her thoughts as well. They were connected, totally and completely. Jonathan had fully awakened senses in Kate she thought had been stuffed away forever.

Allen had snuffed out all the passion that had been so alive in the beginning of their relationship. Kate thought the hurt had gone so deep she might never be able to trust her heart and her feelings to any man again.

Now she was here with Jonathan, wrapped warmly in his arms, listening to the comforting sound of his breathing against her ear. He was asleep. Her world was safe and complete.

If this was all the time she had with Jonathan, if some other twist of fate were to take him away just as mysteriously as he had arrived, at least she would have this moment to cherish. She closed her eyes and drifted to sleep.

Jonathan woke several hours later and smiled as he realized Kate was still snuggled against him. He watched her for a long time, taking in her beauty and the soft sound of her breathing. He smiled as she mumbled in her sleep.

He locked his hands behind his head and stared at the stars visible through an over-sized window in the ceiling which Kate had explained was a 'skylight'. His thoughts turned to the evening of Monica's gallery opening.

Had Margaret been appearing to Kate? Even if it was only her voice? Was she around all the time? Jonathan knew he couldn't see her, couldn't touch her, yet his heart ached for her just the same. She had been taken from him, or rather he had been taken from her at one of the happiest times of both their lives.

But now he was lying beside Kate, and was in love with her. Kate was almost a perfect image of Margaret. How odd that things are passed down through generations. Jonathan remembered his mother telling him that he could have been his Great Uncle Horace's twin.

Jonathan sighed deeply as he took in Kate's beauty once more as she slept. He was in love with two women. How could this be?

He couldn't bear the fact that his beloved Margaret had...passed on. They had planned so much. She told him that she had been secretly choosing the items she would take with her on their elopement, knowing that she might not be welcome in her home after her father discovered she had betrayed his wishes.

Jonathan didn't know why Mr. Hollister was so against his marrying Margaret. Jonathan had access to money, impeccable family history, and would be an excellent father to the many children they had wanted.

He smiled at the memory of Margaret's innocence. She was saving herself for marriage, and although temptation nearly won on several occasions, Margaret had maintained her conviction to have their first night together as man and wife to be very special. When she gave herself to him, it would be as Mrs. Jonathan Wilks.

He played with his pendant absently, remembering the day he arrived in the present time. Strange how he had absolutely no recollection of anything for over one hundred years. Where had he been? Again, he wondered how he had come to this era.

Now that he was here, however, there was a mission to complete. Maybe that was it. Maybe he was some sort of angel on a mission of mercy. No. Preposterous. People can't actually see angels. Or could they?

Regardless, he was here to help Kate. That much he knew. Falling in love was another matter. A potentially disastrous matter.

He had wanted to spend tonight beside Kate, to hold her until she felt better. The incident at the gallery had been a terrible blow, and there was nothing he could do right now to make things right. Somehow he would, if it took everything he had.

But what was he to do about his feelings for her? His heart was telling him to follow this path to Kate. Was it just because she was the image of Margaret? And with Margaret gone, was he just trying to replace her with Kate?

No. That wasn't it. Kate had a genuine warmth of her own. Much like Margaret's, but Kate was a woman of a different time. And he wanted her. He felt a stirring in his lower body as he remembered the events of the past few hours.

Jonathan recalled how Kate had looked as she came out of the bathroom. She had worn no colour on her face—makeup, she had called it—her feet were bare, and she looked positively drained. Yet she was one of the most beautiful women he had ever seen. At that moment, he had wanted to bed her, to take her and release all of the tension that had built up in him, and he suspected, in her over the past few weeks.

He looked up at the stars again, taking in deep breaths, trying to wash away the sensual thoughts that were building. Kate had asked him to stay with her because she was afraid. He understood that, and would put away the notion of spending time with her like this again. Unless, of course, she really needed him.

With a pang of guilt, his thoughts turned to Margaret. Would she always be around them? If he were to stay in this time, would he ever be able to love Kate in the manner he so desired? He closed his eyes and sighed.

A WEEK HAD passed since the break-in. Kate had given a list of the stolen paintings to her insurance agent. It was a significant loss. Ten pieces, plus the computer. A total of twenty-seven thousand dollars.

The police had taken finger print samples, but so far they had not come up with any sure leads on a suspect.

To Kate's relief, the insurance agent was sure she would be covered, but he had asked some very pointed questions, almost accusing Kate of being involved. Kate knew he was just doing his job, but it was still unnerving. She could see the headlines now. "Gallery owner steals own works to settle financial problems."

Thankfully, the bank manager was understanding, and would wait for the insurance check. But she still needed a small miracle to completely pay off the burgeoning debt.

Jonathan had been by her side almost every moment. When he had an assignment to do for Spencer, Kate had gone with him. She felt a surge of pride for him as he interviewed the young participants of the *Summer Winds Children's Art Exhibit*.

He was charming and showed genuine interest as he listened to exhibitors from age seven to seventeen proudly describe their work. Introducing Kate to some of the more talented children, he suggested that if they keep working hard, they may some day have one of their pieces hanging in Kate's gallery in Gastown.

Kate felt a tug at her heart as the children's hopeful eyes shone with Jonathan's suggestion. She had spent so much time burying herself in her work, trying to forget the disappointment of a failed marriage and debt, she had forgotten simple joy. The joy of children's innocence.

Jonathan was smiling at her too. Her stomach tightened. If only he loved her as much as he loved Margaret. If only they knew whether or not he would stay in this time. Kate wanted to spend the rest of her life with Jonathan. To have children with him.

After their trip to the exhibit, Kate wanted to go back to the gallery to catch up on some restoration work she was doing. Jonathan suggested they go for afternoon tea. They stopped in to chat briefly with Jenny, then walked across the street to the Bonbon Café.

As they settled into their seats at a cozy window booth, Kate looked up to see Clarice walking slowly towards them. Her heart stopped. Clarice was staring at Jonathan, a frown etched deeply in her brow.

Chapter 11

JONATHAN TURNED to speak to Kate, but stopped abruptly as he saw the look of concern on her face.

"What's wrong, my love?" he asked, reaching for her hand. At the same time he noticed Clarice, who now stood about four feet from their table, staring at him.

Jonathan looked from the strangely dressed woman to Kate then back to the woman. "Is there something I can do for you, madam?"

She obviously wasn't their waitress, Jonathan surmised. Or if she was, she did not have a lot of skill in friendly service. The frown on her face was very disconcerting. Perhaps that explained Kate's consternation.

"Jonathan," Kate said, squeezing his hand. "This is Clarice. She does tarot card readings here at the café."

Jonathan looked up at Clarice. Why did both women seem so worried? He smiled at Clarice, trying to lighten the mood.

"How nice to meet you, Clarice. Tarot card readings? Is that similar to poetry readings?"

Clarice chuckled. Kate was trying, unsuccessfully, to hide her amusement. Jonathan was bewildered. What had he said?

"Tarot card reading is a type of fortune telling, Jonathan," Kate said.

Jonathan smiled. "Fortune telling? How very interesting." Suddenly he realized the gravity of the situation. If this woman had some sort of powers....

"May I sit with you for a moment?" Clarice asked, already sliding in beside Kate.

They didn't seem to have a choice.

"You are the man I have been seeing," she continued, leaning closer to Jonathan. "You are from a far away place." It was a statement rather than a question.

Jonathan looked at Kate for guidance, but she merely shrugged her shoulders. He didn't know how to respond to Clarice. She was correct in one way—he was from England. But he was also from Gastown, definitely not far away.

"No. It is not a place, it is a time. You are here from a different time," Clarice said flatly. "When were you born?" she asked.

Jonathan saw fear and fascination mingle in Kate's face as Clarice unfolded the secret Kate had tried so hard to contain.

Jonathan stammered, not knowing if he should tell her the truth or not. "I, uh, that is…"

"Jonathan, I don't think there's much point in keeping it from her. She's one of the best known psychics in town," Kate said quietly.

"Eighteen hundred and thirty-seven," Jonathan answered, then waited for a bolt of lightening, or some other reprimand from On High to strike him down.

Clarice just smiled. "Fascinating. What is your name, young man?"

After another brief glance at Kate, he hesitated, then replied, "Jonathan Edward Wilks."

Clarice's smile increased. "I knew it!"

"You knew what?" Kate asked.

"I have been working in this area for many years, as you know," Clarice answered. "There has always been a presence that I could not quite put my finger on. I have been watching your gallery for a long time, before I came to speak with you. I always felt that something wonderful would transpire there. Now I know."

Turning to Jonathan, she continued. "You have been brought here for a very significant reason. Do you know what it is yet?"

"No. Perhaps you could shed some light on that purpose for us, madam."

Clarice smiled again. "You are the painter, are you not?" she asked.

"Well, I do like to paint."

Clarice clapped her hands together. "That is your calling. You didn't have much opportunity to show your true talents before, did you?"

"No. Nobody wanted my paintings." He brightened as he remembered that his old paintings were now worth thousands, and that Mrs. Sumner wanted to buy his new works.

"They will," Clarice said. "You had a great love in the past. Did you know that she is still with you?"

Kate laughed. "No kidding."

Clarice turned to her. "Then you have seen her too?"

"Well, not exactly, but I've heard her speaking to me. When I was a child, and ever since Jonathan arrived, she's appeared a few times. I thought I was going crazy. Clarice, do you know how Jonathan got here?"

Clarice frowned in thought. "Usually there is some kind of key to a time portal. It may just be a place, or it could be something like a talisman. Do you have an heirloom that is special to both of you?" she asked.

Kate looked at Jonathan, thinking about all of the family treasures that she had at home and in the gallery.

The pendant!

Kate reached behind the neckline of her T-shirt and pulled out her half of the coin. "This. This must be what it is," she exclaimed, holding it closer for Clarice to see.

Clarice took the coin as it dangled from the chain. "What is this?"

Jonathan smiled as he extracted the matching half from his shirt. "The other half of this," he supplied, pulling the leather thong over his head and handing Clarice the evidence.

Kate removed her pendant and gave it to Clarice. They both sat back and watched as Clarice put the two halves together.

Jonathan reached over the table and grasped Kate's hand again. Did this strange woman have the answers they were seeking?

"Yes," Clarice said quietly. "I can feel the presence of another woman. There is great love in this coin. This may very well be the key to your presense."

Kate was almost afraid to ask the next question. "Clarice, will Jonathan stay here, in this time?"

Clarice grasped both halves of the coin in her hand. She closed her eyes, not answering for what seemed to Kate like an eternity.

"That, I am not sure of," she answered, looking at Kate with grave concern. "As I told you before, there is danger."

Kate felt her chest tighten. "Danger? But I've already been broken into. I had thousands of dollars worth of art stolen. What more could happen?"

"There, there, my love. Don't worry. I won't let anything happen to you. I promise," Jonathan said calmly, squeezing her hand in reassurance.

Clarice gave them back their pendants. Looking at Jonathan, she said, "I feel the danger is more for Jonathan. But you will be helped by the other woman. She is wearing a long dress."

Kate and Jonathan replied together. "Margaret."

"She is concerned. There is someone who wants to harm you, Jonathan. He is very dangerous. A very angry man. Do you have any enemies here?"

"No. I mean, not that I know of."

"He hasn't been here that long," Kate offered.

Clarice patted his hand. "Just be careful. Normally I do not like to tell people about dark things I see, but I feel you should be warned about this."

"Who do you think it is?" Kate asked, now very concerned for Jonathan's safety. She still didn't like to put a lot of stock into psychic advice, but even she felt a twinge that she couldn't explain.

"It is a man, that is all I know. I cannot see him clearly," Clarice answered, frowning again as if trying to will forward a clearer image.

Clarice rose from the table. "I have said enough. I am very happy to meet you Jonathan. I hope we can have a chance to talk again. Enjoy your lunch."

With that, she walked back to the table she regularly occupied at the back of the cafe.

Before they had a chance to discuss what had just transpired, the waitress came for their order.

Neither spoke, both lost in thought. Finally, Jonathan said, "I was just starting to get used to my life here. In a way, I was hoping that this was truly where I belonged." He looked at Kate, his heart tightening as he realized that he couldn't bear the thought of not being with her.

Kate forced a smile and took his hand. "We just have to take this as it comes. You do belong here. I must say you've done very well at fitting in to this century. Everyone you've met just adores you."

Jonathan squeezed her hand. "Everyone?"

Kate smiled. "Everyone. I'm so glad, for whatever reason, that you showed up at my door. You're a very special person, Jonathan Wilks."

"Westham," he teased. "If I am to stay here, I think we should both get used to my new identity, although I shall miss the old me."

They put Clarice's warning out of their minds during lunch. As they walked back across the street, they saw Mrs. Sumner entering the gallery. She waved warmly as they came closer.

"There you are Kate. And Jonathan, my dear. I must know when I can take that lovely painting home. My living room is just crying for it!" Mrs. Sumner said, bubbling with enthusiasm.

Jonathan bowed slightly and replied, "You shall have it very soon, dear Mrs. Sumner. I shall be honored to have my work in your home."

Mrs. Sumner twittered in return. "Lovely, simply lovely." Turning to Kate as they walked into the gallery, she continued. "Now, Kate. You are the one I specifically came to see. As President of the Vancouver Heritage Society, I would like to be the first to tell you the good news."

Before she continued, Mrs. Sumner noticed Jenny coming down from the upper floor. "Hello, Jenny! How are you?"

Jenny waved at the trio. "Hi, Mrs. Sumner. Here to take Jonathan's painting are you?" she said, smiling teasingly at Kate.

Kate was not amused, and turned back to Mrs. Sumner.

"Good news?" Kate replied. What did the Vancouver Heritage Society have to do with her?

Mrs. Sumner beamed. "We all heard about your most unfortunate incident, and although we know that your insurance should cover most of the losses, we also know that you have been struggling financially."

Kate was stunned, and annoyed. How did Mrs. Sumner know about her financial situation? That information should have been kept strictly confidential by her banker.

"Now, now, dear. Don't be upset. It's not like we were prying, but these things do get around."

Jenny came downstairs and joined the group. She gave Kate a silent message indicating she had not told anyone about what was going on.

Kate suddenly felt ill. She couldn't afford to have people think that her business wasn't doing well. Artists might not be willing to bring their pieces to her if they didn't think she could handle the business of selling their work.

Jonathan also felt the tension radiating from Kate. "What was it you said about some good news, Mrs. Sumner?"

"Oh, yes. Well, the council members have decided, if it's all right with you, Kate, to have the Carston Gallery deemed a heritage building."

Although Kate was pleased to hear the news, as it would mean that the building would never be torn down and replaced by an office tower, she was not sure what that had to do with her financial situation.

"Mrs. Sumner," Kate started, trying to remain calm. "I'm not sure how you came to know about my financial situation, but I don't see how having my gallery designated a heritage building would change anything."

Mrs. Sumner took Kate by the arm, and led her to the sofa. "Please, let's sit down, shall we?"

Now Kate was really worried.

"As you know, I am also a member of the Daughters of Gastown. My ancestors came here about the same time as yours. Anyway, our society would like to put an idea to you that might help your situation, and one that would make all of us proud to be a part of," Mrs. Sumner said, smiling brightly.

"What do you mean, be a part of?" Kate asked.

Jonathan was intrigued. Daughters of Gastown. He wondered if he knew any of Mrs. Sumner's ancestors. He would have to ask her discreetly.

"We want to put together a fund-raising evening, and help you pay off your mortgage on the gallery," she replied, clasping her hands together.

Kate didn't know whether to be flattered, or insulted. She wasn't about to take charity. She got herself into this mess, and she was going to get herself out of it. Besides, she didn't want anyone else to own the gallery. It was hers!

"Mrs. Sumner, I—"

Jonathan cut her off. "What exactly did you have in mind to do for the fund raising, Mrs. Sumner?"

"Oh, it will be such fun!" she replied, her eyes shining with excitement. "We want to have one of those casino nights. You know, black tie, champagne, dinner, then the fun begins. We all agreed that it would be just the thing to help you out!"

Kate sighed. She really did need some help, but she was sure that if she could just sell a few more pieces, things would turn around.

"Mrs. Sumner, thank you for the thought, but I really can handle things on my own. I can't take money from anyone. It just wouldn't be right."

Mrs. Sumner patted her hand. "I knew you would resist the idea. You're just as proud and feisty as your mother was, bless her soul. But it wouldn't just be taking the money."

Kate didn't want to hurt Mrs. Sumner's feelings, but the gallery had been in her family for over one hundred years. She didn't want to have anyone else claiming ownership of it.

As if reading her mind, Mrs. Sumner continued. "It's not like we would be buying it, my dear. All we would like to have is a little plaque on the outside of the entrance noting the name of the Daughters society."

Kate didn't know what to say as her fierce sense of pride began to rise. She wanted to just say thanks for the offer, but she could do it on her own. It was a generous gesture, though. If it meant holding on to the gallery, maybe she should consider it.

"I think it's a wonderful idea, Kate," Margaret's voice whispered in her ear. *"It would be a perfect solution."*

Kate turned her head sharply to the right. There was nothing there except a light scent of jasmine.

Jenny sat on the arm of the sofa, behind Mrs. Sumner, and to the left of Kate. Jonathan stood a few feet away, leaning against the counter of the galley kitchen.

"Are you okay, Kate?" Jenny asked.

Kate felt foolish. She looked up at Jonathan. He was looking at her curiously, then he smiled. It was as if he realized what had happened.

Kate turned to the two women at the other end of the sofa. "Uh, yes. Yes, I'm fine."

Margaret. Kate was beginning to get used to her grandmother's unexpected visits. Maybe this fun-raiser wouldn't be such a bad idea after all.

"I'm sorry, Mrs. Sumner. You were saying something about a plaque."

"Yes, just a small one, you know. Near the doorway."

Jonathan walked over and stood behind Kate, putting a reassuring hand on her shoulder. "I think that would be a splendid idea. It could go on one of the stones in the front archway."

The three women looked at him, confused.

"What archway?" Jenny asked, looking toward the front door.

Jonathan pointed toward the door, making a sweeping curve with his arm. "The stones on the outside, at the entrance. Surely they are big enough to mount a plaque such as Mrs. Sumner is describing?"

"How did you know about the archway, Jonathan?" Mrs. Sumner asked.

Jonathan didn't understand. The stone archway was the pride and joy of Margaret's father. He had had the stones brought in especially for the grand archway.

Mrs. Sumner stood and walked toward the front door. "Kate's father built a covered entrance over the stone archway before Kate was born. He said he wanted to give it a more modern look. How did you know about the former design?"

Jonathan looked back to Kate and Jenny. Both had gone pale. Now he had done it. He had to think fast.

"I, uh, that is, I saw an old photograph of the gallery in one of my tours when I first arrived." He hoped that would be enough to get him out of the frightful mess.

"Is it still there, Kate?" Jenny asked, trying to divert the conversation away from Mrs. Sumner's digging any further.

"I don't know. I never even knew it was there."

Mrs. Sumner answered for her. "Oh, I'm sure it is. As a matter of fact, we could even go further with our fundraiser. Oh, yes. I've just had another wonderful idea."

Kate groaned. This was getting out of hand.

"Mrs. Sumner, I'm really grateful for your suggestion, but I don't think—"

Mrs. Sumner dismissed her with a wave of her diamond-covered hand. "Oh, think nothing of it, my dear. Now as I was saying, what if we took off the wooden exterior and restored the archway, just as it was when the old rooming house was built. We could have people make donations in the amount of, say, one thousand dollars. They could have their name put on a little brass plaque on each stone. A lot of people I know would just love to be a part of this beautiful building."

This was getting worse. Kate felt like she was standing in front of a giant rolling snowball, now out of control. By the smiles on Jenny and Jonathan's faces, she knew she wouldn't get any help in quashing the idea. Not that it was a bad idea, it was just too much.

"Mrs. Sumner, I just don't have the time to organize a function right now, and it would probably cost a lot of money to restore the front entrance."

"Oh, my dear, you wouldn't have to do anything! The Daughters of Gastown would make all the arrangements. All you would have to do is pick yourself out a beautiful dress, get a tuxedo for your handsome escort," she said, waving a hand toward Jonathan, "and come and enjoy yourself. We would do all the rest."

She sat back down on the sofa beside Kate and took her hand. In a more serious tone, she added, "Please. Let us do this for you. For the gallery. We do so want to help."

"Yes, Kate. Do it for our family," Margaret whispered.

Kate shivered at the sound of Margaret's voice. Why couldn't anyone else hear her?

Jenny was nodding. Jonathan beamed. Mrs. Sumner looked imploringly at Kate.

Kate shook her head and laughed. "Okay, okay. You win. Let's have a party!"

Jenny, Mrs. Sumner and Jonathan seemed to all be talking and cheering at once. Kate needed some space. She excused herself, went into her office and closed the door.

She slumped into the chair at her desk and began to swivel, staring at the ornate coved ceiling. Had she made the right decision?

A fundraising casino night. It would probably be a lot of fun, but Kate felt embarrassed at the idea of being the recipient of a charity function. How did her life get so turned around?

Damn you, Allen.

The thought surprised her. Yes, it had been Kate's decision to renovate the gallery, but if it hadn't been for Allen's gambling debts, she wouldn't be drowning in a financial tidal wave.

Kate just hoped that he would stay out of her life from now on. Apart from that phone call, she hadn't heard from him recently. "A blessing," she muttered.

The door opened slowly, and Jonathan poked his head in. "Are you upset, my dear?" he asked.

Kate smiled. "No. I needed a little quiet time to digest what just happened out there. I'm still not so sure it's the right thing to do."

Jonathan came in and closed the door. He sat on the sofa and patted the cushion beside him.

"Come. Sit with me," he said and held his hand out toward her.

Kate sat down and snuggled into his embrace. He kissed her cheek, and hugged her tightly. She wished they were at home. Just the two of them. She wanted to make love to him and make the rest of the world go away.

Jonathan lifted her face to meet his. His kiss was at first gentle, then deepened to light the fire deep within Kate. She wrapped her arms around him, needing to feel him closer.

"Kate," Jonathan whispered.

Kate felt her whole body tingle.

"You are so beautiful," he said, breaking the kiss momentarily.

The sound of Mrs. Sumner's twittering laugh brought them back to the reality of where they were. Kate sat up, and smiled at Jonathan, placing her hand on his cheek. She loved him with all her heart.

"I'd better get back to my best customer," she said, kissing Jonathan lightly and headed for the door.

Kate felt a tinge of guilt as they walked back to the gallery lounge—as if Jenny and Mrs. Sumner had known what was going on in the back room.

"There you are. I was worried I might have scared you off with our plans," Mrs. Sumner teased.

"No," Kate replied. "I just wanted to check on something in my office. I really appreciate what you're doing, Mrs. Sumner. I just didn't want anyone to know that I could use the help, that's all."

"Not to worry, my dear. We understand completely. We'll just tell everyone that the Daughters are helping to maintain a part of our history. No one will know anything else, I assure you."

"So tell me, Mrs. Sumner, what exactly goes on at one of these functions?" Jonathan asked, intrigued by the idea of a gala function.

"Endless fun, that's what goes on," she replied. "Am I right, girls?"

"Absolutely," Jenny answered. "I went to one put on by the Hospital Foundation last year. It was a blast! I actually came out of the evening up a few dollars."

"Up a few dollars?" Jonathan asked. "Are you saying that it is an actual casino?"

"Oh, yes!" Mrs. Sumner said. "First we have cocktails and a lovely dinner, then at about nine o'clock, the casino opens. We have roulette tables, slot machines, blackjack, and my favourite, the craps tables."

"My, my. It does sound exciting. How many people attend such a function?" Jonathan questioned.

"There were at least two hundred people at the one I went to," Jenny recalled.

"And of course, there's also the winner take all game that gets very exciting by the end of the night," Mrs. Sumner added.

Jonathan's interest was particularly piqued now. "Winner take all? What type of game would that be?"

"Why poker, of course," Mrs. Sumner said, smiling brightly.

Chapter 12

THUNK!

The brightly tufted dart hit its mark. "Bulls eye!" Jonathan shouted. "That, I believe, my dear Spencer, would be three in a row. You owe me a pint of beer."

"Scammer," Spencer replied, chuckling as he signaled the waitress for two more drinks.

Jonathan retrieved his darts from the board and the two men settled back on their barstools to take a well-deserved break between games.

Spencer lifted his glass. "Cheers," Jonathan said, as he clinked his glass to Spencer's.

"So, are you ready for the big event this weekend?" Spencer asked.

Jonathan smiled. He really was looking forward to the first black tie event of this new life. He and Kate had gone to the tuxedo shop last week and picked out a very handsome outfit. Jonathan particularly liked the way Kate had looked at him when he came out of the dressing room.

"Yes. It should be rather a lot of fun, wouldn't you say?"

"Yeah. These things are okay, but I hate the penguin suits, to tell you the truth," Spencer replied as he sipped his beer.

"Penguin suits?"

"You know. All the guys walking around looking like they'd rather rip off that noose of a bow tie and just get down to some good clean partying."

Jonathan pondered Spencer's outlook on the event. In his day, whether it be in England or Canada, he supposed most of the men he knew would rather not have to wear a restrictive neck cloth. But that was what was expected of them. Particularly in the social seasons of England.

"By the way, I really liked your last piece. I'll probably run it in about two weeks. Keep up the good work," Spencer complimented Jonathan. "I wasn't sure at first if you could come up with the type of material I needed, but your articles don't need much editing at all."

"Thank you. You know it was awfully good of you to get the newspaper involved as a sponsor for the charity night. Kate is still a bit reluctant to be the recipient of all this, but I think that she'll come around. I think it will work well for everyone involved," Jonathan said.

Spencer nodded as he sipped his beer. Jonathan looked around the cozy neighborhood tavern. It was a far cry from the saloons of early Gastown, although the scene was similar. The main difference was the number of women in the room.

In Gastown, it had only been Haddie's girls that were allowed to spend any time drinking with the men. Oh, occasionally an irate wife would storm into one of the establishments to drag out her overdue husband, but that was rare.

"So, Jonathan. When are you going to ask Kate to marry you?"

Jonathan almost choked on his beer. Sputtering, he replied, "I'm sorry, what did you say?"

Spencer laughed heartily. "You heard me. It's only a matter of time, my friend. Everyone is commenting on you two. It's like you have some kind of karma going on. Don't tell me you haven't thought about it."

Jonathan didn't know what to say. Was it that obvious?

Spencer continued, undaunted by Jonathan's lack of response. "Am I right? Or am I right? Face it buddy. You're hooked, and so is she." He leaned one elbow on the table. "As a matter of fact, I've never seen Kate so happy. It's kinda nice."

KATE LOOKED at her reflection in the large oval mirror of the antique vanity table. She still couldn't believe that tonight's gala event was to help save the gallery. She was grateful for the little miracle that was taking place. Grateful for many things in her life lately. Like Jonathan Edward Wilks Westham.

Kate had begun to feel that he would be a part of her life for a very long time. Every morning for the last month she had woken up with a smile, snuggling into Jonathan's arms as he lay sleeping beside her.

She was an early bird. He liked to sleep. She hated television. He was addicted. He loved the rain. She tolerated it. But she loved him. And she was sure he loved her, although he hadn't come right out and said it yet.

On occasion, Kate still felt insecure with the idea that maybe Jonathan still wanted Margaret, not her. But every time he looked at her across the room at the gallery, or held her hand at the table during dinners, she felt the connection.

It was unlike any other feeling she had ever had with a man. She remembered back to the days when Jonathan first arrived. She had been so afraid to let him near any other people, but he had proven himself to be the perfect gentleman, and any slip-ups were mostly passed off as his being new to the city.

Tonight she would be proud to walk into the party on his arm. Last week at the tuxedo shop, her knees had turned to Jell-O as he had stepped out of the fitting room. He was one of the most handsome men she had ever met. No wonder Margaret had gone against her father's wishes. Jonathan was everything a woman could ask for.

"Kate, darling, it's time to get going," Jonathan called from the living room.

"Be right there," Kate replied as she put on her best perfume. Tonight was going to be very special. She could feel it.

Kate went into the living room to find Jonathan glued to the television set, as usual. She tiptoed up behind him and gave him a quick kiss on his cheek.

Jonathan inhaled the heady scent that enveloped him. He turned to face Kate, and received another kiss on his lips. At that moment, he wished that they didn't have to go out tonight. He wanted to take her. Right here in the living room.

"Ready?" Kate asked, wiping a small smudge of lipstick from his cheek.

"I could think of other things I'd rather do, but that can wait," he replied, rising from the sofa to come around and gather her into his arms possessively.

Kate smiled. "Yes. That can wait. But not for long," she purred.

AS KATE AND Jonathan entered the already humming room at the Pan Pacific ballroom, they were amazed to see the extent of the decor the Daughters of Gastown Society had achieved.

They handed in their tickets at the door, and as one of the ladies checked off their names, the other started to clap and look at Jonathan.

"Congratulations, Jonathan! Your name was drawn as one of the five people to play in tonight's winner-take-all poker game!" she said, excited for him. She handed him a blue poker chip. "This is your official entry marker. Don't lose it now!" she chirped, and turned to the couple who had come in behind them.

Jonathan turned to Kate, beaming from ear to ear. "Marvelous!"

Kate knew that he had his fingers crossed for the last couple of weeks after learning that the only way to play in tonight's big game would be through luck of the draw. Anyone who wanted to participate in the poker game, either men or women, had to send in one end of their ticket with their name on it, and only the five names drawn would play.

"There you are!" Mrs. Sumner bubbled as she gave Kate a warm hug. Waving her hands widely, she asked, "Well? What do you think?"

Kate hugged Mrs. Sumner warmly. "It's absolutely stunning. You ladies have certainly gone above and beyond the call."

She looked at the older woman, trying to reign in her emotions. Once again, Kate was overwhelmed at the generosity being extended to her.

She squeezed Mrs. Sumner's hand. "Thank you so much. I don't know how to repay you for all of this."

Mrs. Sumner twittered in reply. "Oh, think nothing of it dear. We've had an absolutely fabulous time arranging things. It's amazing what kind of memorabilia you can dredge up when needed. Come. Let me show you the *Wall of Time* as we like to call it."

Jonathan's attention piqued. "Wall of Time? That I should like to see," he said, smiling knowingly at Kate.

They followed Mrs. Sumner to the back of the room where posters hung on the wall, showing the growth and changes of Gastown by way of building modifications, fashion trends, and pictures evolving from black and white to color.

"This is one in particular I thought you would enjoy seeing," Mrs. Sumner said, pointing to a two foot by three foot enlarged photo of the front of the gallery, in 1892. It showed very clearly the stone archway Jonathan had referred to.

Along side the picture was an invitation to 'Buy a Piece of Time', by donating one thousand dollars to have one's name or corporation on a brass plaque affixed to one of the stones. There were twenty stones in the arch.

Jonathan leaned close to Kate's ear and whispered, "Just as I remembered it. Quite lovely, wouldn't you say?"

Kate was amazed. She had no idea that the front of her gallery could look so ornate. She couldn't wait to restore it.

They spent the next hour mingling with the crowd, then took their place at a reserved table with other guests of honor. The Mayor of Vancouver and his wife sat across from Kate and Jonathan, along with Mrs. Sumner and her husband, and Spencer and his date, Shareen.

Kate was happy to see everyone enjoying themselves. She began to relax, enjoying the entertainment by singer Long John Baldry, accompanied by the historic Vancouver Firefighters Band, a magnificent fifty-piece orchestra. It was a perfect evening.

Jonathan seemed to be thoroughly enjoying himself as well. He had made quite a few friends over the past couple of months, and mingled with people as if he had known them for years.

Kate could tell, though, that what Jonathan was really looking forward to was the poker game. He had talked about it incessantly for the last few days.

"Finally, I shall have a chance to play a hand or two again," he had said, dreaming of possible riches.

Although Jonathan had been making a steady, but small income from his articles in the *Courier,* Kate knew that he needed more money to feel comfortable in taking care of his own expenses. He had often commented that it was not right for him to be living under her roof without bearing more financial responsibilities.

Perhaps it was time to suggest he start selling more of his paintings. Kate was sure he would jump at the opportunity.

As the band began to play a slow song, Jonathan led Kate through the crowd to the dance floor. He was an excellent dancer, and Kate felt as if she were floating as he expertly guided her around the room in a waltz.

Wrapped in his embrace, their eyes locked. Kate felt they could have been the only ones in the room. The music faded from her consciousness. She was acutely aware of Jonathan. It was as if she was a part of him, and he of her. She could feel love swelling in her so strongly she wanted to cry with happiness.

Jonathan kissed her cheek lightly and Kate nuzzled into the curve of his neck as they danced. She was where she belonged, with the man she loved. Even with the disaster of the break-in at the gallery, Kate felt that her future was positive as long as she had Jonathan.

"Excuse me, may I cut in?"

Kate's stomach lurched. No. It couldn't be. Not tonight.

Jonathan stopped dancing and turned to the person who had tapped him on the shoulder and posed the question. He didn't recognize him. Jonathan suspected the man had already had quite a bit to drink, swaying slightly and smiling oddly as he stood a short distance away.

"Hi, honey," he said looking at Kate. "Mind if I take you off this guy's, uh, hands for a dance or two?"

Kate slid her arm around Jonathan's waist. "Allen. What do you want?"

He held his hands up in defense. "Nothing! A simple dance. Is it a crime for a guy to want to dance with his own wife?" he asked, swaying again.

"*Ex*-wife," Kate said, trying to keep her anger under control. She noticed Jonathan's confusion. "Jonathan, this is my ex-husband, Allen."

Jonathan nodded silently, keeping a protective arm around Kate's shoulder.

"What are you doing here, Allen?" Kate repeated.

Allen frowned slightly, but recovered his false graciousness quickly. "It's a party! I paid for my ticket. I didn't know there was a restriction on who could come," he said acidly. "I'm here to win back some of the money you cost me."

Kate's mouth dropped open in shock. "*I* cost *you*?" she almost shouted. She wanted to hit him. To keep hitting him until all of the anger that she had lived with for two years was expelled. *How dare he!*

She felt Jonathan's hand tighten on her shoulder.

"While I'm sure you would enjoy dancing with this wonderful woman, I believe her dance card has already been filled," Jonathan said, smiling politely at Allen.

Allen stared at Jonathan for a moment, his eyes squinting. "Don't I know you?" he asked, swaying again.

Kate's breath caught in her throat. The photograph of Jonathan and Margaret had been in the gallery ever since they opened it. Allen had probably walked past it hundreds of times. Did he recognize Jonathan?

"I would highly doubt that, old man," Jonathan replied, turning on his English accent. "I've only moved to Canada recently."

"Hmmm," Allen said, still staring at Jonathan. Satisfied for the moment he asked, "So, did you make it into the big game tonight?"

Jonathan nodded. "I did indeed," he replied, holding up his blue poker chip. "As a matter of fact, I intend to win the purse."

Allen laughed maliciously. "Well, put your money where your mouth is, buddy, 'cause *I* will be the one walking away with all the chips tonight." With a wave of his hand, and a last lingering look at Kate, Allen turned and disappeared into the crowd.

Kate shivered. Something was wrong. Why had Allen come here tonight? Of all times to see him again.

Jonathan gathered her into his arms again and continued to dance. Kate leaned her head on Jonathan's shoulder, trying to regain her composure.

Jonathan kissed her temple. "I can feel the tension radiating from you, Kate," he whispered. "Try to relax. I shall not let such a cad ruin the evening for either one of us." Kate lifted her head and he held her gaze. Jonathan smiled warmly. "You know, I think I shall very much enjoy taking every last cent from that despicable man."

Mrs. Sumner signaled the band that she had an announcement, and Long John Baldry politely stepped aside from the microphone as she approached. A few couples had stayed on the dance floor in anticipation of the next song, but most people were already heading towards the gaming room, which was about to be opened.

As Mrs. Sumner gave a round of thanks to everyone for coming, and to the sponsors, a partition in the grand ballroom began to open, gliding noiselessly on its tracks. Once again, the crowd ooh'd and aah'd at the wonderful decor that the Ladies of Gastown had created. It almost felt like an authentic old saloon.

Kate watched Jonathan's reaction as they entered the gaming room area. She could see the warmth of nostalgic remembering, mixed with regret on his face. Maybe he hadn't adjusted quite as well as she had thought.

"Marvelous," he said quietly, smiling as he looked around at the decorations. Turning to Kate, he offered his arm. "Shall we?" His smile always melted Kate. She took his arm with both hands as they wandered about the room, deciding which game they would play first. It would be a while yet before the big poker game started.

Kate was enjoying herself. She had stopped worrying about the idea of accepting charity to help her out with her financial troubles. Everyone here was having a good time, and she would still remain the official owner of the gallery.

By the time the call was made for the poker players to assemble, Jonathan and Kate had played several rounds of roulette and craps. Their luck had held and they were up twenty dollars.

Jonathan settled into a chair at the green, felt-covered table. It was a familiar feeling, though the setting very different from the last time he had played. He took out his precious savings of five hundred dollars and bought chips. Although his stomach was churning with nervous excitement, he tried to maintain an outward calm. He suspected that this lot of players was of an elite gambling set, much stiffer competition than he had ever faced in the smoky back room of the Deighton Hotel.

Jonathan glanced over at the *Wall of Time*, which featured a blown-up photograph of Gassy Jack's saloon. He smiled and shook his head, still amazed that he had come to find himself in this time, claiming a completely new identity and fooling everyone in the process.

Kate stood behind him, her hands resting lightly on his shoulders. Once the dealer announced the game was about to start, Kate gave him a reassuring squeeze, a kiss on the cheek for luck, and told him she was going to mingle some more while he played. He watched her graceful gait as she walked back to the main dining area. She was so beautiful.

Jonathan was sure his luck would hold out for everything now. His job with Spencer, selling his paintings, and hopefully, for the big game tonight. He looked at the first hand dealt to him, smiled inwardly, and discarded two. Yes, he was a lucky man.

KATE OCCASIONALLY looked toward the poker table, but tried to stay away. She didn't want to interrupt Jonathan's concentration. Not that she was sure it would make any difference, never having played poker herself, but this was Jonathan's big night. He had been so looking forward to it. Kate was quite content to visit with the local dignitaries that had come to the gala. It gave her a subtle opportunity to promote the gallery, and perhaps acquire some new clients.

She wandered over to the photograph of the archway in front of the Hollister Rooming House. All but one of the plaques had been spoken for. Amazing.

Even though she was in that building every day, she wondered what it would have been like to live there. She smiled, knowing it was where Jonathan had once lived. Where he had first come in contact with her family.

She glanced over at him again. He was smoking a cigar, his 'poker face' firmly in place. Earlier that week, he let it slip that he had been making an extra effort to practice his poker face, so that he might have a better chance at winning in the big game. Kate sighed. She loved him so very much.

Suddenly she smelled jasmine. She listened for the now familiar voice, but the band had started playing again, and was drowning out any regular conversation. Just the same, she knew Margaret was there.

THREE HOURS later, Kate wandered back to the poker table. The last two times she had checked, Jonathan's pile of chips had been maintaining its height, but now it had dwindled. His poker face had turned to intense concentration.

Kate looked at Allen. His pile was even smaller than Jonathan's. He had removed his coat and loosened his tie. He was perspiring heavily, and was more intoxicated that when he had approached them on the dance floor. Kate gave Jonathan's shoulder one more reassuring squeeze and walked back to the main room.

It was after midnight, and quite a few of the guests had already called it a night. Both Long John Baldry and the Firefighters Band had wrapped up, and a lone DJ was doing the music. The lights reflecting off the glitter ball swirled around an almost empty dance floor.

Kate sat at a table with Mrs. Sumner, who despite the hour, was still alive with energy. She looked past Kate and beamed.

"Jonathan! Is the game over already?" she asked, frowning.

Jonathan sighed as he stopped behind Kate's chair and stuffed his hands into his pockets. "I'm afraid it is for me, Mrs. Sumner. Lady luck was just not with me tonight." He looked down at Kate, hoping she wouldn't be too disappointed.

Kate reached up and held on to Jonathan's arm. She gave him a reassuring smile. It didn't matter to her whether he won or lost. The money wouldn't have made much difference at this point. The only thing Kate had really wanted was for him to have had fun, to feel like he belonged in this time. Belonged with her.

She turned to Mrs. Sumner. "Are you sure you don't want some help cleaning up, Mrs. Sumner? I'd be happy to pitch in."

Mrs. Sumner waved her away with a twitter. "Oh, heavens no. The hotel staff will take everything down. All we have to do is some paperwork to tally up the evening, and our committee is already at work doing that. No, you two run along. It's been a wonderful night, and I'm sure you'll be happy with the results, Kate dear."

Kate felt like crying. Nobody had ever done something so grand for her. She leaned over and hugged Mrs. Sumner warmly. "How can I ever thank you for all that you've done?" Kate said, her voice choked with emotion.

Mrs. Sumner smiled, looking from Kate to Jonathan, and back to Kate. "Be happy, my dear. Your mother, and your grandmother, rest their souls, would want that for you. And I think Jonathan is just the person to make that happen." She turned and walked away before Kate could reply.

Jonathan slipped his arm over Kate's shoulders, and gently turned her toward the exit doors. "Come on, let's go for a walk."

They rode silently in the ornate brass elevator to the main floor, and walked outside to the promenade deck surrounding the hotel and Vancouver's Convention Center on the shores of Burrard Inlet. Several cruise ships were docked around the complex.

Jonathan and Kate planned an imaginary trip, sailing into some exotic Caribbean port. They chose Holland America's *Westerdam* from the four ships in port, deciding it had the best pool.

As they reached the front of the building, they noticed the moonlight shining across the water. It was a beautiful, crisp autumn night, yet still quite warm. Jonathan stood behind Kate and wrapped his arms around her. She leaned into him, closing her eyes and taking in the peacefulness that surrounded them.

His mind wandered back to the night he had asked Margaret to marry him, on this same shore. Jonathan knew that it was time once again. Time to take a stand and set a new course. If he was to stay here, he wanted sure his life and Kate's would be the very best it could be.

He turned her around to face him. Her eyes shone with love as she smiled at him, and Jonathan knew his fate was forever sealed.

Taking a deep breath, he asked, "Kate, my darling Kate, will you—"
"There you are, you lousy, cheating card shark!" boomed a man's voice from the shadows.

Chapter 13

KATE AND Jonathan whirled around toward the voice. Kate gasped as she saw Allen staggering toward them, barely able to stand, let alone walk straight. She felt Jonathan's arms tighten around her protectively.

Kate was livid. Was he ever going to stop making her life a living hell?

"Allen, get out of here and leave us alone!" she shouted, unable to contain her anger.

Allen wobbled closer then stopped, trying to maintain his balance as the contents of the glass he held sloshed over his hand and sleeve. "This guy's going to pay, Kate. He stole all my money," he slurred.

Calmly, Jonathan took his own stand. "My good man, if you recall, I too ended up with no money at the end of the night, so I fail to see how you could come to such a ridiculous conclusion."

"Well, aren't we just a saint, mister la-te-da? You think you're so damn superior 'cause you're living in *my house,* with *my wife!*"

"Allen, shut up!" Kate demanded, trying to keep her voice down as another couple strolled by. "Go crawl back where you came from before I call the police."

Allen raised his hand that held the drink, once again spilling the contents on himself, and with one finger, pointed at her and sneered, "You can't tell me what to do. If it wasn't for me, you would have never got that stupid gallery of yours off the ground, and you know it!"

Kate was about to launch into him again, when Jonathan intervened. "I think it's been a long night, and it's time we should all go home. I'll thank you to keep your distance from Kate, Allen, old boy, or you'll have to answer to me."

Just as Jonathan began to guide Kate past him, Allen threw his drink on the deck. The crash of splintering glass against concrete echoed through the quiet night air. Kate screamed and jumped away from the flying debris.

Jonathan spun around to face Allen, the closely capped lid on his temper disappearing. "Now see here, you blithering idiot!" he shouted angrily, but before he could say another word, Allen lunged at him, growling like a madman.

Jonathan was caught off guard as Allen grabbed him by the lapels of his tuxedo and slammed him into the steel railing. Kate heard a sickening grunt erupt from Jonathan as the impact knocked the wind out of him. As if in a dream, she screamed, feeling paralyzed, not knowing how to help Jonathan.

He'll be okay, my dear. He is very strong.

Kate looked around frantically, Margaret's voice still ringing in her ears.

"Margaret, help him!" Kate pleaded, as Allen landed a solid punch in Jonathan's stomach.

"Hey! What the hell is going on?" Kate heard another man shouting. She spun around to see Spencer running full speed toward Jonathan and Allen.

Without hesitation, he grabbed Allen by the shoulders and roughly yanked him away from Jonathan, who was still bent over from the force of the blow. Allen tried to run away, but Spencer tripped him mid-stride, and as Allen stumbled, Spencer pushed him down to the cold cement, pinning his arm behind him.

Kate heard the pounding of heavy footsteps behind her again, and turned to see two hotel security men running toward the foray. They immediately pulled Spencer off Allen, and as Allen made a feeble attempt to run again, they grabbed him, forcing him against the wall of the hotel.

One of the security guards still had a firm grip on Spencer. Jonathan, still slightly out of breath, quickly set the guard straight on who was the perpetrator, and the guard let go of Spencer.

Kate ran into Jonathan's arms, holding on tightly as the guards radioed for the police to attend the scene.

Although still shaken, and breathing raggedly, Jonathan asked, "Are you all right darling?"

Kate just nodded, her head buried against his chest. She was trying so hard not to cry. It had been such a beautiful evening. Why did it have to be spoiled by her drunken ex-husband?

Moments later, the police arrived. After taking statements from everyone, they escorted Allen, handcuffed and still ranting, to their patrol car. The quiet sounds of the night surrounded them again.

Jonathan extended his right hand to Spencer, as he kept his other arm firmly around Kate's shoulders. "I am in your debt, Spencer, old boy."

Spencer shook Jonathan's hand briefly. "No problem. I was just walking through the lobby to the pay phone when I looked out the window and saw that S.O.B. deck you."

Spencer looked at Kate and frowned. She seemed more tired than he had seen her in the past few weeks, and she was shivering. "Come on you two. Let's get out of this night air. Kate, honey, you look like you need to go home and crawl into a warm bed. What were you guys doing out here, taking a romantic moonlight stroll?"

Jonathan smiled. "As a matter of fact we were. Indeed, I was just about to ask Kate," he started, once again turning Kate by the shoulders to face him, "if she would do me the honor of becoming my wife?"

Kate's mouth dropped open briefly, then turned into a bright smile. She threw her arms around Jonathan's neck, and he lifted her off her feet, twirling her around and around in the shadows.

When Jonathan gently placed her back on her feet, he noticed Spencer standing quietly watching them, beaming from ear to ear as well.

"I gather that's a 'yes'," Spencer said, laughing. He stepped forward to hug Kate, then pumped Jonathan's hand. "Congratulations. Now can I say 'I told you so'?"

JONATHAN glanced at the ornate steam clock on Water Street, one of the biggest tourist attractions in the Gastown area. It was about to go off, sending plumes of steam into the air as it whistled out the Westminster chime tune. Eleven o'clock. He had one hour to do some shopping before he met Spencer for their weekly luncheon.

What had started as a meeting to discuss potential story ideas for Jonathan had turned into a ritual. More often than not, their time had been spent trying to best each other at a game or two of darts, although Spencer seemed to have an endless well of subjects for Jonathan to write about. While Jonathan still had to concentrate during their conversations so as not to reveal his true identity, he felt comfortable with the friendship developing between himself and Spencer.

Today, however, Jonathan was on a special assignment. He had saved enough money from his last few writing assignments to put a deposit on a ring of engagement for Kate. He had browsed through two stores already, but had not yet seen anything befitting her style and grace.

Jonathan wanted only the best for Kate, even though his income was still very limited. A ring of engagement was something to be cherished, and not just any one would do. He looked across the cobblestone street at the luxurious brass and glass door of Monari Jewellers, noting the carved granite plaque at the entrance which read "*Since 1895*".

He smiled. An odd feeling came over him as he looked at the date inscribed in stone. Here he was, in 2007. Technically, he never made it to 1895, but seeing the date was somehow comforting. He walked across the street, pulled open the heavy door and entered the quiet plushness of the store.

As he wandered past the cases of sparkling gold and diamond jewelry, a display in the corner of the store caught his eye. It was china tea sets, with a sign at the top of the case that read 'Collectibles'. There were several teapots, some quite similar to those that Kate used daily in the gallery and at home.

As Jonathan admired the fine workmanship of the hand painted pieces, a sales clerk approached him.

"They really are quite exquisite, aren't they?" she asked, smiling politely.

Jonathan returned her smile as he picked up one of the items, carefully turning it over to reveal the stamp on the bottom. It read, "Devon, England". Not far from where he had once lived.

"Yes. Yes they are," he replied, carefully placing the teapot back in its spot.

The woman continued, picking up one of the other pieces. "This one was just brought in recently. We have the matching cups and saucers on the way," she offered. "This particular set is one of a kind. Imported from England in the late 1800's. Are you familiar with antique china?" she asked.

Stifling a smile, Jonathan nodded. "Yes, I'm familiar with a lot of items from that time, but these are much nicer than most I've seen."

The woman continued her sales pitch. "You have a keen eye for quality. This set is valued at over three thousand dollars."

Jonathan was taken aback. Three thousand dollars for a tea set? "My goodness, madam, that is quite a sum of money," he answered, thinking of all the pieces Kate had at home and the gallery. Were her pieces worth just as much? Did she even know the possible value of her collection?

"Is there something in particular that you were looking for, sir?" the woman asked, hopeful for a sale.

"No, just doing a spot of browsing. I thank you for this most interesting information. Perhaps I shall drop by again to see more of the collection," he said. With a courteous nod he turned to leave. "Good day, madam," he said in his clipped English accent as he walked to the door.

Jonathan decided to go to the pub directly and wait for Spencer. He ordered a pint of Guinness. He was finally developing a taste for modern day ale, although he yearned for a tall glass of the best from old England. He opened the small, laminated menu but the words just swam in front of his eyes. His mind wandered back to the jewelry store.

His latest discovery could be of great importance to Kate indeed. Even though the fundraising party had been a huge success, and Kate no longer had to worry about paying the bank for her gallery, she should know if her collection of china had significant value.

Three thousand dollars! For a tea set! Jonathan smiled and shook his head. Who would have ever dreamed? Had he known that such simple items would fetch such a large sum in this time, he would have....

He shook his head. If fate had not brought him to this time, he would have been long since dead. But someone else had seen the value of importing fine china from his beloved England. And had prospered from doing so, even if it was over one hundred years ago.

Donovan Trueman.

Jonathan felt his blood boil, even at the thought of the man's name. He was the one who ultimately won the delicate hand of Margaret. Jonathan's heart ached, knowing that he had not been able to give Margaret all that she had dreamed of. Had not had the privilege of growing old with her, to be the father of her children.

Had she really felt the same for him? Had Margaret's heart kept Jonathan's memory with her? Even though Kate had told him that the letter found with Margaret's half of the coin told of the great love they had together, did she marry Trueman out of duty alone? Had she waited for him to return? Had she thought of him throughout her life? He would never really know.

Jonathan was startled out of his thoughts as Spencer slapped him on the back and slid into the opposite chair.

"Hey, pal. You're here early, aren't you? I thought you were going shopping for Kate's ring today," Spencer noted as he opened his menu.

"Yes, I did, but I haven't found anything suitable as yet. I did make an amazing discovery, though."

"What's that?" Spencer asked, not looking up from his menu.

"I was over at Monari's Jewellers, and they had a display of china tea sets imported from England."

Spencer signaled the waitress for a beer, then turned his attention back to Jonathan. "So? Most upper-end stores like that sell expensive china."

"But these pieces were noted as being 'Collectibles', and they were from the eighteen hundreds. Do you have any idea how much they are worth?" Jonathan asked, leaning forward in his chair.

Spencer smiled. "Well, not being the delicate china kind of guy, no. I have no idea."

"Three thousand dollars. For one little tea set," Jonathan replied slowly, emphasizing each word.

Spencer's eyebrows raised in surprise. "Wow. Do you have some back home in England that you're thinking of flogging over here?"

"No, but have you not noticed how many pieces Kate has? She may be sitting on a veritable fortune." Reluctantly, Jonathan brought up the subject of Donovan Trueman. "Are you aware that Kate's distant grandfather imported china back in the eighteen hundreds? She told me that's how he made his fortune in old Gastown."

They were interrupted briefly as the waitress placed Spencer's beer on the table, and took their order.

Spencer took a sip of beer, then sat back in his chair and smiled. "I smell a story here."

"What do you mean?"

"Why don't you do some research and come up with a story about early businessmen in Gastown. There were probably a lot of items imported from Europe. You can focus the article on Kate's great-grandfather—do a story on his success.

Jonathan's jaw clenched. Do a story to herald the success of the man who cheated everyone in Gastown? The cad that never had a penny to his name? The one who lived the life that Jonathan should have had? The thought was quite revolting. However, he was being given an assignment, and he really had no excuse to turn it down.

JONATHAN returned to the gallery immediately after his lunch with Spencer. Although he was eager to talk to Kate about the possibility of the great value of her china collection, he was reluctant to tell her about his new assignment. Of course, as Spencer had pointed out, he had a wealth of research resource at his fingertips in Kate. He would not have to through a single history book to write the article. All he had to do was ask Kate to tell him about Donovan Trueman.

The thought sickened him, quite frankly. Donovan Trueman was and always would be a cad in Jonathan's mind. How could he convincingly write an article about the man's success as a businessman, without every word bringing back vivid memories of his past?

Jonathan stopped short of the front entrance to the gallery. His past was just that. The past. Now he was a contributing member of a new world. Kate's world. He would just have to do his assignment and put the past where it belonged.

Taking a deep breath, he pushed the door open and walked in. "Kate, darling, are you here?" he called.

"Up here," she replied. "In the studio."

Jonathan took the stairs two at a time. Peering around the corner into the room where he and Kate had both set up easels, he found her working on restoring a large, rather ugly painting.

He crossed the room and stood behind her, bending over to kiss her lightly on the top of her head. "Not my taste, love, but I'm sure someone will buy it."

Kate stopped working and sat back to study the painting. "Yes. Rather garish isn't it," she drawled in a fake English accent. "So, how was your lunch with Spencer? Scintillating conversation? Or did you just play darts all afternoon, as usual?"

Slumping into a nearby chair, Jonathan pressed his hand to his chest in mock indignation. "My dear, you wound me. Have I not proven myself to you to be a worthy writer? A wizard of words?"

Kate smiled, rolling her eyes. "I'm sure you'll live. So, did he have any new assignments for you?"

Jonathan leaned forward and rested his arms on his knees. "As a matter of fact, my love, I have had a most interesting day. Are you aware that your lovely collection of china teapots, and their accessories may be worth quite a sum of money?"

Kate continued working on the painting. "I suppose they could be. Why? What have you discovered now?"

Jonathan recounted the story of his trip to Monari's and his conversation with Spencer. As he talked, Kate put down her brush and began to listen intently.

"So, your assignment is my Grandfather Trueman?"

Jonathan groaned. He hated that name. "Not exactly. He would be a part of it, but the larger portion of the article would be on valuable antique tea sets. Do you have any other pieces, besides what I've seen here or at home?"

"Sure. There are two trunks full of china in the attic. I don't think anyone has used them in years, if they were ever used in the first place. I'm sure they're all in mint condition. I wonder how much they would be worth? Not that I have any intention of selling them. They are a part of my family's history," Kate noted. She took her brushes to the cleaning jars and wiped her hands on a clean rag. "Come on. Let's go upstairs and see what's there."

Kate climbed the narrow stairway to the attic. The old, original door creaked loudly as she pushed it open. Sunlight streamed through a small, oval, stained glass window on the south side of the building. Particles of dust rose and swirled lazily in the musty air as Kate wound her way through a maze of forgotten pieces of her history.

"This place is a mess. I really should get up here and do something about it one day." Kate went to the farthest corner of the attic, dimly lit by the single light bulb in the centre of the attic ceiling. She bent down and looked at a faded tag on an old steamer trunk.

Jonathan was amazed. Trinkets of generations past lay before him. How many of the items had belonged to Margaret, if any? It was not proper for a man to enter a lady's boudoir in his day, unless of course the lady was one's wife. Was the comb and brush set that lay on the old table by the wall the one Margaret had used? Did she sit at her dressing table, brushing her hair, thinking of him?

He was jolted away from his thoughts as Kate apparently found what she was looking for.

"Aha! Here it is," she said triumphantly. "I don't think anyone has opened this trunk for literally decades. This is kind of exciting, don't you think?" she asked as Jonathan helped remove the boxes that sat atop the trunk.

Jonathan had to admit it was exciting. He was opening a piece of Kate's family history, but more intriguing was the fact that it was another connection, however remote, to Margaret.

Not that he was holding on to her. His life now was completely centered around Kate. He was in love with Kate, and nothing could diminish that. But he still yearned for the aspects of who he was only a few short months ago, at least in his memory.

They began to take out the carefully wrapped pieces of china. There were several complete sets in the first trunk.

"According to the woman in the jewelry store, one of the sets was worth three thousand dollars. You could be sitting on a small fortune here, my dear."

Kate set an ornate cup on its saucer and sat back on her heels to observe the collection. "They really are quite beautiful, aren't they? Are there any more pieces in there?"

Jonathan looked into the trunk, noticing two small bundles left in the bottom corner. As he reached for the last piece, he heard a slight tearing noise. What had looked like a piece of tissue was a corner of the trunk lining, and it lifted away as he took out the wrapped china.

"What was that noise?" Kate asked, standing to peer into the darkness of the trunk. "Jonathan, look. There's something sticking out of the lining."

Jonathan noticed the piece of paper to which Kate was referring, and carefully pulled it out of the ornate lining. In faded black ink, his own name stared back at him.

To Jonathan Wilks.

Chapter 14

JONATHAN LOOKED at Kate, completely dumbfounded. What could it possibly be? But he recognized Margaret's delicate penmanship right away.

"Open it, Jonathan," Kate urged quietly.

His hands shook visibly as he turned the envelope over and gently opened the flap. Once more, he stopped and looked to Kate. She nodded in encouragement.

The paper was quite brittle, but not yellowed. Jonathan's stomach clenched so tightly he thought he might be ill. On one hand, he was overcome with excitement, on the other, he was shaking with fear at what the letter may contain.

Carefully, he unfolded the pages. His throat constricted as he saw line after line of Margaret's handwriting. His eyes misted slightly, blurring the words.

Kate placed her hand gently on his shoulder. "I'll leave you alone to read it. Tea will be ready when you decide to come downstairs," she said as she walked toward the door.

Jonathan looked across the room and noticed the shaft of light pouring through the octagonal stained glass window. Taking a deep breath, he stood and crossed the room, carefully side stepping the myriad of boxes and old furniture. Dust particles danced and swirled in the sunshine as he sat in the circle of light.

Taking another deep breath, he began to read.

July 17, 1873
My Darling Jonathan,
It has now been five years since you went away. I still miss you so very much. I don't know where you are, or why you left, but I do know that you would not break my heart intentionally. I can only hope that you are all right and that there is a reason for you leaving me. I am writing this letter in hopes that some day, even if I am no longer alive, it will find its way to you. There are some things I would like to tell you about, to convince you that my love for you never faltered.

On the morning you disappeared, I thought I would die. I had a very bad dream during the night that something had happened to you, but when

I awoke, and heard the birds singing, saw the sun shining brightly, I thought it would be a wonderful day after all.

I began to worry when you did not come down for breakfast. I knocked on your door, and hearing no response, I feared something was wrong. I went into your room and saw that your bed had not been slept in. I tried to find out where you were, but my father said he had not seen you since the evening before, when you were at the Deighton Hotel.

Darling Jonathan, I know that you would never have left me on the day of our elopement. Later that afternoon, your hat was found floating in Burrard Inlet. They told me you were dead, that you had been partaking of whiskey at the saloon, and that you must have wandered too close to the water and fallen in. They said the tide most surely swept you out to sea.

Even though I could never accept the fact that you were gone, a part of me died that afternoon, Jonathan. My life no longer had meaning without you. I prayed every night that it was all just a bad dream, that you would walk through the front door one day and tell me that it was all a lark. Of course, if you did that, you must realize that I would be very angry for such a prank. But not for long. You are my one and only. I will never love anyone such as I do you.

I want to explain to you why my life went on in the direction it has. I waited as long as I could, but my father insisted that I marry, that the age of twenty-three was unthinkable for a daughter of his to be unwed. There were several suitors, but since Donovan Trueman had come into such a large inheritance, my father convinced me that he would be the best possible choice for a husband. But I never loved him, Jonathan. You must believe me when I say that no one will ever replace you.

I did my best to hide all of your belongings, all of your wonderful paintings. Every chance I had, when Donovan and the children were out of the house, I would go to the attic and take out one of your pieces. It was almost like having you here with me again. I loved to watch you paint. When you thought I was reading my books, on those wonderful days we would picnic by the river, I watched you. I watched your strong arms create images so lovely. I was the happiest woman alive on those days, Jonathan. Nothing will ever erase these memories I hold so dearly in my heart.

When I look at my four children, as much as I love them, my heart aches. They could have been your sons and daughters. But if this letter finds its way to you, at least you will know that I never stopped thinking of you. Never stopped loving you. Perhaps one day, if you do not return to me in body, we will be together again in the heavens. This is my greatest wish. Until then, you will always be on my mind, and in my heart. I love

you, Jonathan Edward Wilks.
  Forever yours, darling,
  Margaret

JONATHAN STARED at her name on the bottom of the page. Minute after minute ticked by in the silence of the attic. His mind was numb. Tears welled in his eyes, and he was thankful no one else was around to witness his emotional state.

She had waited for him. Waited until it was no longer possible to stand up to her forceful father's wishes. He would do anything to erase the pain she must have gone through in those months after he disappeared. A pain he shared, particularly on the day he arrived here, when Kate had told him that his beloved Margaret had long since died. He felt a part of him die that day, just as Margaret had said of her feelings on the day of his disappearance. But all he could do now was hope that, as Margaret wished, he would meet with her again in the heavens. A love as strong as they had must surely be eternal.

Jonathan took another deep breath as his thoughts turned to Kate. It was kind of her to leave him on his own to read the letter. She was now as dear to him as Margaret had been. He loved Kate completely. Yet his heart still ached for Margaret. Would that ever change?

How strange it was that he was still alive, over one hundred and thirty years after he had last spoken to Margaret. Was this a phenomenon of modern life, or was he unique? The thought had never occurred to him before. Perhaps there were others in this bustling city that held the same secret as he. He laughed and shook his head. Perhaps if there were, he could start one of those support groups as he had observed on the television shows. "My name is Jonathan and I'm from the past." He laughed again.

Then he looked at the letter in his hand. His mood sobered immediately, but his heart did not feel as heavy. He was thankful to have Kate. Jonathan suddenly realized that she must be greatly concerned about the contents of the letter.

Jonathan stood and quickly made his way to the attic door. He needed to see Kate.

KATE BUSIED herself with mundane tasks as time ticked by, excruciatingly slow. The better part of an hour had passed, she noted as she glanced at the grandfather clock.

Staring at the clock, she felt an odd sensation come over her, like she was looking at it for the first time. It really was a beautiful piece of workmanship. Margaret's family must have been thrilled when it had arrived.

Kate looked expectantly to the top of the stairs. She wondered if Jonathan was okay. He had been absolutely stunned to see his name on that envelope. So had she for that matter. Why hadn't anyone ever noticed it before? Perhaps neither her mother or any of her grandmothers had ever dug deep enough in that particular trunk. After all, one family can only use so many teapots, and Lord knows there were enough in the heirloom collection to serve tea to the entire Royal family.

She looked upstairs again. Still no sign of him. When the phone rang, Kate jumped, startled out of her thoughts. She answered it, still watching for Jonathan.

"Hi Kate. How are ya?" Spencer asked, sounding as chipper as ever. The man never seemed to be in a bad mood.

"Hi, Spence. Fine, and you?" she replied.

"Never better! Is Jonathan there? I'd like to go over a couple of changes to this week's piece."

"Yes he is, but he's tied up at the moment. Can I get him to call you?" Kate offered, not wanting to disturb Jonathan. She was sure he wouldn't be in the mood to discuss editorial details at the moment.

"Sure. I'll be at the office till five. Hey, did he tell you about the idea for a story on Donovan Trueman?" Spencer asked, excitement clearly showing in his voice.

"Yes. As a matter of fact, that's what he's doing right now. We opened a couple of trunks in the attic and he's going over some pieces in the collection," Kate answered.

"Great! Do you think you could fill in some info on your great grandfather, or I guess he would be your great, great grandfather?"

"I'm sure I could come up with a story or two," Kate said, knowing that Donovan Trueman was the last person Jonathan would want to learn more about, especially now.

"Great," Spencer repeated. "Okay, just have him call me when he's got a minute. Gotta go. See ya."

"Bye, Spence." Kate hung up the phone and looked upstairs again. Jonathan stood at the railing, an unreadable expression on his face as he studied Kate silently.

"Hi," Kate said softly. "Are you okay?"

Jonathan smiled weakly and started down the stairs. Kate wanted to rush over to him, to wrap her arms around him and take away the pain he must be feeling. But she stood in place, watching as he neared her. He still hadn't said a word.

She suddenly had a sinking feeling in her stomach. Had the letter affected him to the point that he couldn't, or didn't want to marry her now? Did he realize that his love for Margaret was so strong that he could never fully give himself to another woman? Not even to her?

Jonathan stopped in front of Kate and placed his hands on her shoulders, his eyes never leaving hers. Still he said nothing. Kate's heart hammered against her ribs.

"You are so very beautiful," he said quietly, and gently drew her into his embrace.

Kate let out a long breath she hadn't even realized she was holding. Wrapping her arms around his waist, she buried her face in his shoulder.

They stood that way for several minutes, neither one speaking. Kate wanted, needed to know how he was feeling, yet at the same time, she was petrified what he might say.

Finally he spoke, his mouth close to Kate's ear. "I love you, Kate Carston. I love you with all of my heart and soul."

Kate lifted her head from Jonathan's shoulder and met his gaze. She could see the love there, and knew, at that moment, everything would be fine.

Tears of happiness welled in her eyes. "I love you so much," she whispered, lifting up on her toes to kiss him softly on the cheek.

Jonathan took her face in both hands, a broad smile lighting his face. "Kate, my love, will you still do me the distinct honor of becoming my wife?"

"Yes, Jonathan, I will still marry you," Kate said, laughing as she felt her fears float away. Silently she thanked Margaret. For what, she didn't know, but it seemed the right thing to do.

SIX WEEKS had passed in the blink of an eye. Kate was walking on a cloud and felt like she had only just met Jonathan yesterday, instead of months ago.

How strange that she was with the man she had always dreamed about, even though for most of her life he was nothing more than a black and white image on the walls of her family home.

She didn't care any more how he got to her back door on that fateful day. In one more week, she would be walking down an outdoor aisle in Stanley Park, celebrating the change of season, and the start of her new life as the wife of Jonathan Edward Wilks Westham.

Kate hoped that Margaret was happy for her. Jonathan had been everything to Margaret, even after his disappearance, and now Kate couldn't imagine her world without him.

Her mind wandered back to the sweet hours that they had made love and talked last night. Never had she felt so cared for. In the early morning light, she had just watched him sleep. He was her prince. And soon he would be her husband.

A light tap on the door brought her out of her daydream. Jenny came into the office, two coffees in hand. She smiled at Kate as she handed her one of the cups.

"It's so great to see you in love again," she said warmly.

"Not again," Kate replied, wrapping her hands around the mug. "I have never felt like this. When I married Allen, I think it was more a sense of that was what I was supposed to do. Jonathan makes me feel so alive!"

Jenny smiled. "That's pretty obvious. I'm so happy for you. Both of you. He's really special, besides the fact that he's, uh, a little different."

Kate gazed out the window, her thoughts turning to the quiet wedding ceremony they had planned. A horse and carriage ride through the park to a secluded garden behind the Stanley Park Pavilion. If the weather turned, they would move everything indoors, but Kate hoped with all her heart that they could go ahead with their 'back to nature' wedding as Spencer had dubbed it.

Spencer would be Jonathan's best man, and Jenny would be Kate's maid of honor. Jenny and Spencer had gone to great lengths to plan the traditional stag nights. They had decided to do them on the same night, but would make sure that neither group would go to the same place.

Kate was really looking forward to tonight's festivities. Neither she nor Jonathan knew where they were being taken, but the plan was to meet back at the gallery by midnight, then they would go home together.

BY SEVEN o'clock, the gallery was buzzing with men and women mingling, getting ready for their night on the town, each trying to guess where the other group was going. Only Spencer and Jenny knew the exact agenda and they weren't telling anyone.

They had decided to have everyone meet at a central place, have a glass of champagne to toast the future bride and groom, then start the parties.

As six cabs pulled up in front of the gallery, signaling the guests it was time to set off for their adventures, Jonathan sought out Kate in the crowd.

He pulled her into his arms and kissed her firmly. She responded eagerly, not caring who witnessed their show of affection.

"Hey, come on, you two. Can't you wait till the honeymoon? We've got ground to cover tonight," teased Spencer, tugging at Jonathan's sleeve.

Kate let go of Jonathan, blowing him another kiss as the group of men pulled him toward the waiting cabs.

Jenny stood at the front door, encouraging the women to follow suit. "Come on, ladies. We have some serious partying to do ourselves." A chorus of hoots erupted as the women headed to the remaining cabs.

MARGARET NERVOUSLY twisted the delicate linen handkerchief in her hands as she watched the last of the cabs pull away. It wouldn't be long now. She was happy that part of her mission had been completed. The deed to the gallery was safely in Kate's vault. Nobody would ever take it away from her now. Their family home was safe.

But there was more to come. Part of her hoped that things would go her way, but for Kate's sake, Margaret wanted the outcome to be to otherwise. The decision would have to be made by Jonathan, though. The final result would depend purely on his heart.

Margaret looked around the room. There had been so much love through the generations that lived and worked in this house. She walked over to the wall where one of Jonathan's paintings hung among other historic pictures of Gastown. She smiled sadly, and wondered what her life would have been like if they had been able to follow through with their plans.

She knew it was never meant to be. But, depending on the outcome of the next few hours, she might have her chance to be with him again.

JONATHAN WAVED to the remaining partygoers as he and Spencer headed toward the door and their waiting cab.

It had been different that he expected. Bar-hopping was not something that he had ever experienced, but suffice it to say, he had enjoyed himself immensely. It had been a little inconvenient to walk around all night with a plastic ball and chain affixed to his ankle, but he supposed it added to the folly of the evening.

He couldn't wait to get back to the gallery, to meet Kate. He would tell her about most of the events they had participated in, however, there were one or two incidences he felt he should keep to himself. Definitely not suitable tales for a lady.

As they settled into the back seat of the cab, Spencer gave Jonathan a hard nudge on the shoulder. "Well, buddy, one more week and you're toast," he teased, his voice slightly slurred.

Jonathan looked over at Spencer. He felt pleasantly relaxed as the rounds of Jack Daniels caught up with him. "What ever do you mean? In one more week, I will be marrying the most beautiful woman in the city.

In fact, in the world. And right now, as we speak, that angel is waiting for me at the gallery," he said, closing his eyes and resting his numb head against the side of the cab.

Sitting up with a start, he turned to Spencer, leaning close to his face. "I love her with all of my heart, you know."

Spencer laughed and pushed Jonathan back to his side of the cab. "No kidding. Nobody would have ever known."

The cab stopped at a red light near the corner of the alley behind the gallery. "This is fine, my good man. I shall walk the rest of the way," Jonathan instructed the driver. "Goodnight, Spencer. And thank you for a splendid evening indeed."

"Hey, no problem. Give Katie a hug for me, will ya?"

"Hey, no problem," Jonathan parroted, shaking Spencer's hand. The cab drove away, and Jonathan waited for three more cars to pass before he crossed the road and started down the alley to the back door of the gallery.

As he neared the gallery, two men stepped out of a neighboring doorway and stopped him. Startled, he stumbled backward a few steps. A man standing in the shadows of the building called out to the two men who had kept Jonathan from reaching the door.

"That's him," said the man. Jonathan could not see his face, but immediately recognized the voice.

Allen.

One of the men in front of Jonathan pushed him back against the brick wall. Jonathan's heart pounded against his ribs. Every instinct rang of danger. Allen's voice came from the shadows again.

"Hey! I'm not paying you to dance with him!" he snarled angrily.

Jonathan turned toward Allen's voice. He could no longer see him, but Jonathan knew he was still there.

"Look, Allen, I have done nothing to you. If you have a problem with me then I think—"

The sound of a gunshot shattered the night air, echoing against the buildings in the alley.

Chapter 15

JONATHAN FELL to the ground, a searing pain shooting through his chest. The sound of the gun still reverberated in his ears. The realization that he had been shot sunk in as his mind whirled. He was going to die.

No! No! Not yet! Help me! Someone, please help me!

His mind screamed out for help, but he could not summon the strength to make a sound. Kate. She would find him here like this. She would be devastated. He couldn't do that to her. He just couldn't put her through the same anguish Margaret had suffered.

"She will be fine, Jonathan. Don't worry," a woman's voice said softly.

Jonathan recognized the voice immediately. It was coming from behind him, and suddenly Jonathan realized he was standing on the shores of Burrard Inlet. All of the city noise had disappeared. In fact, the city had disappeared. This was where he had proposed marriage.

She was sitting on a rock near the water's edge, smiling that angelic smile he fell in love with so very many years ago. Except it didn't seem like years ago. He felt every bit as much in the present here as he did five minutes ago, lying on the cold cobblestones of the alley.

"Margaret. My Lord, Margaret, is it really you?" he asked, unsure if she was an apparition that would vanish.

She stood and went to him, the folds of her long dress swishing as she walked. She opened her arms as she neared Jonathan, and he quickly drew her into his embrace, holding on tightly as if to keep her from ever going away.

He took her by the shoulders, looked into her eyes for a long moment, then lowered his head to brush his lips against hers. She tasted like sweet honey. Every emotion associated with Margaret that he had bottled up in the past few months erupted. Losing all control, he deepened the kiss, feeling her body pull closer to his, her mouth opening to take his exploring tongue.

His love for Margaret had never been stronger. She was every bit as exciting and loving as Kate. It was as if time had never stopped, or as if everything he had experienced recently was a dream.

Kate!

Jonathan suddenly pulled away from the heat of the kiss and stepped back. Holding Margaret by the shoulders, he looked at her. Really looked at her. It was amazing. She and Kate could be sisters.

"Margaret. What is happening to me? Was it all a dream?"

She smiled as she took his hand, leading him over to a log. "Come, Jonathan, sit with me. No, it wasn't a dream. I have been there with you all the time. But for tonight, let's just be together. You will find your path soon enough."

Jonathan was totally confused, but trusted her word. As the waters of the inlet lapped against the shore, he gathered Margaret into his arms, and closed his eyes. He had missed her so very much.

He noticed she was not wearing the pendant. "Margaret, my love, you are not wearing your half of the coin. Did you not put it on today?"

"Jonathan, I never took it off until the day I married Donovan. Even then, every day I took it out of the velvet bag I made and put it on, just for a moment or two. Just to feel your love. But now Kate is wearing it. It is where it belongs."

"Margaret, what is happening? Please, my love, I must know. Am I finally...dead?" he asked, not really wanting to hear the answer.

"No, Jonathan, you have not died. Yet. It will be up to you to make a choice soon as to where you want to continue your life. But not now." Pointing down, she said, "Look, my darling, I prepared your favourite foods, just for this special evening."

Jonathan noticed the picnic basket at their feet, a yellow gingham cloth covering the contents just as it had on every outing they had shared. He felt totally relaxed, as if he belonged here once again. He wanted to enjoy their time together, as precious now as it had been all along.

KATE SLUMPED on to the sofa in the gallery lounge, kicking off her shoes and putting her feet up on the rectangular, oak coffee table.

"Hey, feet off the table, young lady," Jenny scolded in a motherly, but joking tone. She poured tea into two glasses that contained Gran Marnier and Amaretto.

"It's *my table,* in *my gallery* and I can put my feet any where I darn well please," Kate replied, smiling as she leaned her head back against the sofa and closed her eyes.

Tonight had been a lot of fun. The highlight of the evening was seeing Mrs. Sumner do the Macarena dance with the no-neck doorman at the Pump House Tavern.

Now Kate and Jenny were back at the gallery, waiting for Jonathan. They decided to make Blueberry Teas for a nightcap. Kate felt giddy, not only from the champagne they had consumed throughout the night, but from sheer joy. Her life was perfect, and she couldn't be happier.

Her state of calm was short lived as they heard what sounded like gunshots coming from the back of the gallery. Kate sat up quickly and stared at Jenny, who was holding the teapot and staring back at Kate, just as astonished.

"Was that what I think it was?" asked Jenny apprehensively.

Kate's stomach clenched with fear. The sound had come from directly behind the gallery. "Quick. Call the police," Kate said as she headed to the back door.

Jenny picked up the cordless phone and dialed 9-1-1, her hands trembling.

Kate stood at the back door and listened, afraid to open the door in case there was still some crazy person with a gun outside. After what seemed like an eternity, she saw the flashing red and blue lights of a patrol car through the frosted back windows. Jenny was right behind her as she undid the security chain and cautiously opened the back door.

A police officer was bent over someone lying in the alley. *Please, God, let Jonathan still be out at his party*, Kate prayed. As she stepped out of the doorway, another officer cautioned her to stay back.

An ambulance arrived, and the paramedics quickly retrieved their medical equipment.

"What happened?" Kate asked, trying to see past the officer. A paramedic was now kneeling beside the man on the ground. As he stood to get a piece of equipment, Kate's worst fears were realized.

"No!" she screamed. "Please, God, no!" She pushed past the officer and rushed toward Jonathan, panic setting in deeper as she saw the front of his shirt completely soaked with blood. One of the officers grabbed Kate by the arms, telling her to stay back.

Kate tore away from his grip and dropped to her knees in front of Jonathan. She took his face in her hands, desperate to hear him speak, to open his eyes, to give her any sign that he was alive.

"Jonathan! Jonathan, look at me! Please! Sweetheart, open your eyes," she begged, tears streaming down her face.

Kate felt someone tugging at her. Vaguely she heard Jenny's voice mixed with the police officer's. They were trying to get her away from Jonathan, but she couldn't. She couldn't lose him. If she let go of him, he might disappear. Reluctantly, she let Jenny take her back a few steps as the paramedics worked. She felt numb.

"I've got a pulse, pretty weak though. Bullet wound to the left upper chest. Let's get him in. Stat. Notify for a trauma team," the paramedic instructed his partner.

Kate hadn't realized she had been holding her breath until she heard them say he was still alive. She started to shake uncontrollably, her legs becoming weak. She couldn't lose him. Not now. Not ever.

Jenny was holding on to her. "He'll be okay, Kate. He'll be okay. Don't worry."

The paramedics worked quickly, carefully strapping Jonathan to a spine board, then moving him to a stretcher. An oxygen mask had been secured over his face, and with the help of the police officers, they lifted Jonathan into the ambulance.

Kate ran forward. "I'm going with him!" she cried, heading for the back of the ambulance.

"Sorry, ma'am, I'm afraid we can't allow that. We're taking him to Vancouver Hospital. Do you have someone who can give you a ride there?" the paramedic asked, taking a wet cloth from the ambulance. "Here. You'd better wipe off that blood."

Kate looked down at her shaking hands. They were covered with Jonathan's blood. Everything started to spin. She was going to faint.

"Be strong, Kate. Jonathan needs your strength right now. Go to the hospital. He needs you to be there at the hospital for him," Margaret insisted. *She hoped Kate could hear her through the shock that was setting in.*

"I'll get her there," Jenny responded to the paramedic, taking the cloth and wiping the blood from Kate's hands. The look on Kate's face scared Jenny. She was in shock. Jenny turned to the police officer. "We were at a party tonight, so I can't drive."

"I'm going to need a statement from both of you, so I can give you a ride to the hospital," he replied, his voice professionally void of emotion in the turmoil that surrounded them.

"I'll just get our purses and lock up. Kate, are you going to be okay for a couple of minutes?" Jenny asked, afraid to let go of Kate's trembling body.

Kate looked at her and nodded silently. The officer took Kate by the arm and guided her to the patrol car, opened the back door and helped her in.

As she sat in the back seat of the police car, Kate gazed out the window at the buzz of activity. She felt lightheaded, like the whole thing was a scene from a movie. None of it seemed real.

"Yes, Kate, it is real."

Kate spun around. A woman sat beside her in the back seat. It was almost like looking in a mirror, but the woman was wearing a long dress.

"Margaret?" Kate asked breathlessly.

Margaret smiled. "I thought it was time we got acquainted a little more formally. Although we have talked on several occasions. I enjoyed myself immensely all those years ago at your tea parties in the attic."

Kate wasn't sure what to do. The jasmine scent was strong, somehow comforting. Was she going to die too? Was Margaret an angel who was preparing her for the next step? She had to know.

"Margaret, what is going to happen to Jonathan? Is he going to die? Was he only here to help me save the gallery, and now that it's mine, is he going to go away?"

Margaret laughed. "Dear child, so many questions. I cannot tell you at the moment what is to come. That decision will be up to Jonathan. I can tell you that he loves you very much."

"But he loved you just as much before he, uh, came here. Margaret, where was he for all of those years? He doesn't remember a thing."

Margaret placed her hand over Kate's firmly-clasped hands. Kate pulled back slightly as she realized that she could see Margaret's hand on hers, but all she felt was the same wisp of warm air she had felt across her arms the other times. Was Margaret really there with her?

"We all have a purpose in life, my dear. Sometimes it takes more than one generation of life to conclude our mission. Jonathan was just waiting for the time to be right to complete his."

"So he's going away," Kate said softly, tears welling up in her eyes. "He's completed what he came here for and now he's going away." Kate buried her face in her hands, unable to hold back her fears and the overwhelming emotions of the situation.

"Hey, it's going to be fine. He'll make it."

Kate felt Jenny's warm hug and heard her reassurances. Kate pulled her hands away from her face, seeing only Jenny in the back seat with her. The police officer got in and started to drive out of the alley.

Kate frantically looked around the inside of the car.

"Katie! Hey, what's wrong? What are you looking for?" Jenny asked, concerned by Kate's odd reaction.

Kate stopped suddenly, looked at Jenny and realized that she must have been hallucinating. Shaking her head, she grabbed Jenny's hand. Answering feebly through her tears, she replied, "Nothing. I was just, uh, I...nothing. He can't die, Jen. He just can't."

She started to cry again. Jenny handed Kate a tissue, trying to convince her that things really would be fine.

Five minutes later they reached the hospital. Kate noticed the ambulance was empty. Jonathan was already inside. Kate ran across the tiled entrance, barely waiting for the automatic doors to the emergency room to open. She could hear the officer and Jenny calling for her to slow down, but she had to get to Jonathan. He had to be alive.

Kate ran up to the desk. "I'm here to see Jonathan Westham," she said anxiously.

"You'll have to take a seat in the waiting area, ma'am," the nurse instructed calmly. "The doctors are attending to him now."

Jenny had caught up to Kate and took her by the arm. "Come on, you can't do anything. Besides, the police want to ask us a few questions," she urged, guiding Kate toward a chair in the crowded waiting room.

The police officer, Constable Drake, motioned to Jenny he would talk to them in another room, away from the noise and confusion.

As they settled into the hard, utility chairs in the small room off the waiting area, Constable Drake opened his notebook. He asked Kate and Jenny to recap everything they had done, and what they heard before calling for help.

He wrote down detail after detail as both Kate and Jenny added pieces to the events of the evening.

"Do you know if Jonathan had any enemies, anyone who would do this?" the officer questioned, looking from Kate to Jenny.

Kate frowned. Why would anyone want to hurt Jonathan? He didn't even know that many people. He was one of the most polite, generous men she knew.

"Maybe he was just in the wrong place at the wrong time?" Kate suggested, hoping that there wasn't someone who would purposely cause harm to such a loving man.

"It's possible, but his wallet was still in his pocket, and the paramedic said he mumbled something on the ride in. Something about the alley, or they weren't sure if he was trying to say somebody's name."

Kate and Jenny looked at each other, realization suddenly coming to both of them. "Allen," they said in unison.

"Pardon?"

"Allen Brigham. My ex-husband. He attacked Jonathan three weeks ago after a charity function for the gallery. He was drunk and blamed Jonathan for his loss at the charity poker game," Kate explained. Her fear was rapidly changing to cold fury. If Allen had anything to do with this, she would do everything in her power to see him put away for a very long time.

"Did he threaten Jonathan as well?" Drake asked, still writing.

Kate thought back to that night. "Yes, he did. As the officers were taking him away in handcuffs, he was very angry. He yelled, 'I'll get you, you damn foreigner! Nobody takes away what belongs to me!' The officers told Allen to shut up. Then they pushed him into the back of their car."

Officer Drake looked at Kate and smiled. "Thank you, Miss Carston. I'll pull the details of that night and talk to the officers on duty. It may be nothing, but from what you've given me, and the report from that night, we'll see if there's any connection. We'll be in touch," he said, standing as he put his notebook into his shirt pocket. "Try not to worry. I'm sure they're doing everything they can."

Kate smiled feebly. "Thanks. I know."

A doctor came out of the emergency room and leaned over the admitting desk, talking briefly to the nurse. Kate saw her point in their direction, and the doctor nodded. His face was somber as he approached Kate.

"Are you Kate Carston?" he asked, flipping through the chart in his hand.

Kate stood quickly, holding on to the back of the chair to support her still wobbly legs. "Yes. Please. Is Jonathan going to be all right?"

"We're not out of the woods yet, I'm afraid. He'll be heading into surgery right away. He's lost a lot of blood."

Kate's legs gave way, and she collapsed into the hard chair again. Jenny put a consoling arm around Kate's shoulders. "I can't believe this is happening," she uttered weakly.

"What's his condition at the moment?" Jenny asked.

"He's critical, I'm afraid. The bullet went in just below his collarbone. It pierced part of his lung and hit an artery in his left shoulder, which cut off oxygen to the brain. I'm afraid he's in a coma."

"No. Please dear God, no." Kate pleaded, her hands shaking uncontrollably as she covered her face, tears once again flowing.

Jenny stayed with Kate through the night. They were escorted to a more comfortable waiting room where Kate paced for four hours, stopping to stare down the hall at the doors marked 'No Admittance'.

She held on to her pendant like a lifeline, hoping she could somehow send Jonathan a secret message. Kate looked over at Jenny, asleep on the sofa. By the time Jonathan was taken in for surgery, it was one o'clock in the morning. The nurses had brought out two blankets for them, but Kate couldn't sleep a wink. It was almost five o'clock now.

She walked to the water cooler and poured herself a cup. She drank as if she had just come off of a month long trek through the desert. She filled the cup again, needing something to take her mind off the terrible situation she was facing.

What if Jonathan didn't come back to her? Maybe he was never supposed to have asked her to marry him in the first place. Maybe he was supposed to be with Margaret through eternity. Maybe he had just been sent here for a short time, like a guardian angel, and they were never meant to fall in love.

But she was in love with him. Totally and completely.

Kate stretched out on the long sofa and pulled a blanket over her. She knew she wouldn't sleep, but she felt chilled. Probably from the stress of the night's events. She closed her eyes. Maybe if she just rested for a minute or two, her head would stop throbbing.

JONATHAN finished the last of the bread and cheese that Margaret had packed, and drank the rest of his wine. It had been a most enjoyable evening, sitting on the shore with the moon shining brightly on the water.

They talked of how Margaret's life had unfolded. How her children had been her greatest joy, as were her grandchildren. Every time Jonathan had approached the topic of why he was here, with Margaret, she would change the subject. Finally, he felt he must have an answer.

"Margaret, dear, I must know what is to become of me. Where do I belong? I am having the same feelings now as I did when I was first sent over from England."

Margaret dabbed at the corners of her mouth daintily with a white linen napkin, as she finished a piece of raisin pie. "Tell me, Jonathan. Do you find your life with Kate interesting?"

Jonathan thought for a moment, not sure if the answer would be upsetting to Margaret. "Well, actually, yes. I mean, at first there were quite a few problems. But I have a job, you know. A real job. As a writer. Imagine, Margaret. I, Jonathan Wilks, a writer. Somehow I think even my father would have approved of that choice of occupation."

Margaret smiled, stoking his face lovingly as he rested his head on her lap. "Yes, I'm sure he would. Jonathan, only you can decide if you want to go back and live your life with Kate. The option is available to you."

Jonathan took her hand and brought it to his lips, lightly kissing the soft skin of her palm. "I'm confused, Margaret. I love you very much, and the thought of spending my life with you is what we had planned for so long."

"Yes, I know, but I had my life. You have yet to live yours completely. Kate loves you, and she is terrified of losing you, but only you can make the choice. You have been given a true gift, Jonathan. The opportunity to live what might be termed as two lives."

He studied her face, wanting to memorize every detail. "If I choose to go back to Kate, will I ever see you again?" he asked.

"Perhaps, but not for a very long time. You have a full life ahead of you, if you choose. I love you, Jonathan Edward Wilks, or should I say Westham," she teased. *More seriously she added, "But I also love Kate. I want her to be happy, too."*

Jonathan closed his eyes and sighed. It was a heavy decision.

Chapter 16

TWO DAYS had passed. Kate never left the hospital during Jonathan's surgery, and had been at his side since the moment they brought him into the Intensive Care Unit.

Jenny had gone to Kate's condo to get her some changes of clothes. Spencer came in daily to check Jonathan's progress.

Although Kate appreciated all their help and support, she was concentrating on Jonathan. She sat beside his bed, holding his hand, watching for even the smallest sign that he was coming out of the coma. That he would be coming back to her.

She remembered the vision she had seen in the back of the police car. Margaret had told her the decision would be up to Jonathan. Kate knew how much he loved Margaret, but she was also sure, with all her heart, that he loved her.

Was it a question of loving one more than the other? Would that be the only criteria for Jonathan living, and spending his life with Kate, or dying and continuing on with Margaret?

Shortly after Jonathan had been brought to the ICU, Kate had taken his pendant, which the nurses had removed when he was admitted, and put it back over his head. He looked so peaceful, except for the cluster of machines that monitored his vital signs.

Perhaps it was up to her to let go. Maybe it was selfish of her to want Jonathan to stay. After all, he had only been here for a few months. He had already planned a lifetime with Margaret before fate had taken him away.

Kate took his hand in hers, watching him as he slept. The doctors had told her he was very lucky. If the bullet had landed two inches lower, he would definitely not be here. As it was, he had suffered extensive internal bleeding and a punctured lung. They said Jonathan must have a very strong will to live, if he had survived so far under these circumstances. If he made it through the next seventy-two hours, he would probably be out of danger.

"Please, Jonathan, give me some kind of sign. Squeeze my hand, just a little. Please let me know that you are in there." She waited, watching for any sign she could hold on to as a thread of hope.

But there was nothing. She brought Jonathan's hand to her cheek as her tears flowed. Maybe it was time to let go. Maybe he needed a sign from her that it was okay to move on with his life.

Kate stood beside the bed and looked down at Jonathan, his long black hair splayed against the pillow. Even now, hooked up to the machines, his shoulder and chest bandaged heavily, he was a magnificent man.

She thought of her favourite poster that had hung in her bedroom as a teenager. It had read, 'If you love something set it free. If it comes back, it's yours. If it doesn't, it never was'.

"I love you Jonathan. If you want to go to Margaret, I'll understand," Kate whispered as she bent over and kissed him.

Still nothing happened.

Kate's eyes felt heavy. What sleep she had managed to get in the past few days had been fraught with dreams, almost nightmares of being lost in an unfamiliar city. She had been searching for Jonathan, calling his name over and over, but he was gone.

It was almost midnight and the ward was very quiet. Only the occasional whispering of night duty nurses nearby broke the still air.

Kate gazed at Jonathan, praying for some kind of miracle to wake him from his coma. She thought she saw him move, and sat up quickly, but what she had seen was not a movement, but a—transformation.

Kate shook her head, blinked several times, then rubbed her tired eyes, trying to focus on what she thought she was witnessing.

She could see through him!

The blanket still formed over his body, but his arms, his head and his chest were completely translucent. The wrinkled, cotton bed sheets, the printed stamp of the hospital logo on the corner of the pillowcase, were visible through Jonathan. Kate's entire body tensed. She opened her mouth to scream but she could not utter a single sound.

She whirled around to the nurses. They were busy doing paperwork, totally oblivious to what was happening to Jonathan.

Maybe it was Kate who was not seeing things right. She quickly turned her attention back to Jonathan. She could still see through him. What was going on?

Kate reached out to touch his hand. She could feel him just as much as she had not five minutes before. This was it. He had completed some kind of angelic duty, and now it was time for him to go away, to wherever it was he had been for the last century.

As much as she knew it was not her choice to make, Kate cried out softly as she leaned her forehead on Jonathan's hand.

"Please don't leave me. I love you so much, Jonathan."

She didn't look up again. As long as she could feel Jonathan's hand in hers, she knew he was still there. If she looked up and saw that he was still fading, Kate knew she might lose him.

Kate sniffled and let out a short, wry laugh, keeping her head buried against the blanket and Jonathan's hand. "Thanks a lot Jonathan," she whispered. "If you're going to leave me for another woman, did it have to be one of my relatives?"

"Well, well, well. Will you look at that," said a nurse from the doorway.

Kate's breath lodged in her throat. She was afraid to look up. How was she going to explain this to the nurse? Kate was sure they had patients that 'disappeared' on occasion but—

"Welcome back, Mr. Westham," the nurse said brightly as she walked toward the bed.

Kate's head snapped up. Jonathan was looking at her, smiling weakly. She could no longer see through him.

Their eyes locked for the first time since the night of the shooting. The connection was unmistakable. Kate felt it to the core of her soul.

Kate jumped up from her chair. "Jonathan! Oh, Jonathan!" She took his stubbled face in her hands and gently kissed him. She drew back for a moment, looking over the entire length of his body, wondering if she had imagined what she had seen. Then she kissed him again. And again. And again. His smile grew with each kiss, almost as if he was being energized.

He tried to talk, but was only able to utter a raspy squeak.

"Save your energy. There'll be plenty of time to talk," the nurse said with authority. "I'll go find Dr. Dudley." She looked at Kate and winked. "Try to keep him in bed will you?"

"I saw her," Jonathan whispered.

"I know. I saw her too," Kate replied. "Does that mean that you are going to go to her? Are you done here?" Kate asked cautiously.

For a long moment, Jonathan didn't answer. He just stared into Kate's eyes, a half smile barely formed.

Kate's heart sank. He was trying to think of the best way to let her down easy. She broke her the gaze they held.

She felt him squeeze her hand weakly, she looked back at him. He tried to speak, but again, nothing but a ragged noise emerged. He swallowed hard, licked his dry lips, and tried again.

"I love you, Kate," he whispered. "I'm not going anywhere. Will you still marry me?"

Kate started to cry. Jonathan frowned, a look of fear on his face. Kate lifted Jonathan's hand to her face, her tears pooling between her cheek and his fingers.

When she smiled through her tears, she saw Jonathan's expression relax. "Of course I'll still marry you, Jonathan Edward Wilks Westham."

IT WAS OVER a week before the doctors released Jonathan, with strict instructions that he must have complete bed-rest for at least a two weeks. Therefore, the wedding had to be postponed. A minor detail, considering what they had both been through. Kate and Jonathan decided that a New Year's Eve wedding would be a wonderful way to celebrate their new life together.

Two days before he went home, Kate happily informed Jonathan that Allen had been arrested for attempted murder, and all of the stolen items from the gallery had been recovered in Allen's apartment.

By the second week of convalescing, Jonathan had insisted on accompanying Kate to the gallery. September was now almost over, and the crisp smell of fall was in the air. Jonathan reveled in the joy of being alive, watching the leaves turn, and drinking in the beauty of Kate.

Kate was behind on a restoration project, and had wanted to get an early start, so they picked up breakfast on the way to the gallery. The sun was just rising over the city when they sat down in the gallery lounge to enjoy their chocolate croissants.

Although Kate and Jonathan had talked briefly about his experience with Margaret, neither of them brought up the topic of whether he was to stay permanently in Kate's time. For over a week, Kate had been summoning the courage to ask him.

Leaning forward on the sofa, teacup in hand, Kate took a deep breath and said, "Jonathan. There's still one thing that we don't know the answer to. Or at least, I don't."

Jonathan's hand stopped mid-way to reaching for his second croissant. "What would that be, my love?"

"We still don't know whether you are here to stay, I mean, in this time. Do we?"

Jonathan took Kate's cup from her hand and placed it on the coffee table. Gently, he pulled her to him, wrapping his arms protectively around her.

"I guess, like any other couple, we are just going to have to take our chances. I don't have any idea how we shall know either way, other than the fact that I am here. It would seem to me that, at least for the foreseeable future, I am yours, Kate. Would that be all right with you?"

Kate laughed softly. "Oh, I think I could put up with you for a decade or two longer."

Something beside the staircase caught Jonathan's attention. "Look at the beautiful colours."

The sun had risen to a point where its beams shone through the stained glass window above the front door, throwing a wonderful rainbow display against the white wall.

"Amazing," Kate whispered. "I don't think I've ever noticed the colours being so bright before."

Suddenly, two shadows appeared to blot out a part of the image. Jonathan and Kate looked at each other, then looked toward the window. Nothing was blocking the suns rays coming through the stained glass. What were those shadows?

"Jonathan! Look!" Kate cried.

The two shadows seemed to be coming into focus. Once having no shape, they seemed now to be two half-circles with jagged edges, exactly like their pendants. The two jagged sides faced each other, and slowly floated together.

Jonathan and Kate were stunned. They stood and walked toward the stairs. What were they witnessing? Then the familiar smell of jasmine filled the room. This time Jonathan also noticed it.

"Margaret!" they said in unison.

"Jonathan, she's giving us a sign," Kate said, taking her necklace off and holding it out in front of her, the half coin dangling in the air.

Jonathan followed suit, and before their eyes, the two halves of the coin joined, seemingly of their own accord. The scent of jasmine grew stronger, and a faint glow surrounded the merging halves.

Kate reached for the coin, and was astonished to see that the two halves were now one—fused together, with only a zigzag line left to show it had ever been taken apart.

As the jasmine scent began to fade, Kate stepped into Jonathan's waiting embrace. Time was on their side now.

~ * ~

Laurie Jones

Laurie took a giant leap of faith in 1997 and stepped out of the corporate world to follow her writing passion. She is now living her dream, making her own hours as a freelance writer, and working on the constant flow of ideas for magazine articles, film and the world of romance, including the screen adaptation of COLORS OF TIME.

Laurie looks forward to the day when she can relax on the deck of a West Coast waterfront home, take in the beautiful sunsets, and share the moments with special people in her life. Write to Laurie at conceptsunlimited@telus.net.

Printed in the United States
96394LV00001B/4-153/A